THE RECLUSE

JENIKA SNOW

THE RECLUSE

By Jenika Snow

www.JenikaSnow.com

Jenika_Snow@Yahoo.com

Copyright © November 2020 by Jenika Snow

First E-book Publication: November 2020

Photographer: Wander Aguiar

Cover Model: Peter P.

Photo provided by: Wander Book Club

Cover Designer: Designs by Dana

Editor: Kayla Robichaux

Proofreader: All Encompassing Books

They said I was crazy for taking a job for a recluse billionaire in the middle of nowhere.

I said it was a reprieve from the world and myself.

Cooking and cleaning for Finland "Fin" Hawthorne at his secluded estate situated on a hundred acres seemed like just the recharge I needed. No interaction with society, the vast wilderness as my backyard, and the likelihood of having to actually socialize with my new employer was slim to none.

That sounded like the perfect escape to me.

He said he liked his space, his privacy. He told me he hoped I liked being alone the majority of the time. Fine by me.

And then I meet Fin face-to-face. He's rough around the edges, callous, and aloof, not to mention he's a gorgeous towering behemoth of a man. And one look at him had me imagining being thrown over his shoulder as he took me to his room and devoured me.

I shouldn't want my employer, but when my boss

looked like him... no one with a beating heart could deny the brutal attraction that poured off Fin.

Right away, I didn't miss how he always seemed to be where I was. I saw the way he watched me constantly, tracking me with his eyes like he was starving and I was the only thing that could sate his hunger.

And God did I want to be his meal.

I was playing a dangerous game, but knowing I could unravel a man like Fin made it all the more enticing.

Kitty

Everyone told me this was a mistake, that taking a job as a live-in cook and housekeeper for a man—a billionaire recluse—who lived out in the middle of nowhere was the worst mistake I'd ever make. They told me I'd regret it, that I was leaving my friends and family. They said I was selfish for wanting to disconnect.

Maybe they were right, but at twenty-two years old, I felt far too old for my age. I felt like I'd been disconnected for so long already. I felt like they were wrong and this decision was the absolute best one I'd made in a long time. Because it was for me. There were no expectations for this job except cooking edible meals and cleaning one man's house.

No trying to excel at school. No trying to make people happy, to laugh at stupid jokes or always put on a smile. No trying to convince my parents that just because I didn't have a boyfriend—that I'd never had one—didn't mean there was something wrong with me.

College wasn't working out, the city life was too hectic and consuming for me, and I just wanted to escape to breathe. I had no intent to make this a lifelong career, tending to a billionaire's domestic affairs, but for a short while, it seemed like it would be a good reprieve. It would be mindless work that could let me focus on so many unimportant things.

Maybe my mind could start to heal from the toxicity that surrounded me from the world.

To be honest, I hadn't even expected to get the job. I had no experience with professional domestic duties and had no references to back up that I was this incredible worker who wouldn't disappoint.

I'd even been brutally honest in my application, and maybe it was that honesty that had gotten me the job. I'd written that my life was too busy, that the prospect of disconnecting seemed like euphoria. I'd been blunt, not really catering, admitting I needed this reprieve. It had only depressed me more.

I also noted that I didn't want to make this my life's mission, that this wasn't a career for me. And it was because of that honesty that I really thought I'd be overlooked, seemed unprofessional and not a good fit.

But then I'd gotten an email saying the job was mine.

Relocation fees included.

A sign-bonus included.

Room and board provided.

Weekly paychecks directly deposited into my account.

Honestly? It sounded too good to be true, and I was waiting for the catch.

A big part of me assumed that my new employer was probably the biggest asshole to ever walk the face of the earth. And after doing a quick internet search, trying to confirm my suspicions, all I'd come up with was that Finland Hawthorne was as mysterious as he was aloof. He was quiet, as he was disengaged with society.

Antisocial was what he'd been called many times.

But that worked well for me.

Maybe it would be like my own little oasis, a vacation where I never actually had to see my employer, where I did my job, got paid, and I wouldn't have to worry about pleasing anyone face-to-face.

I turned onto the dirt road, the GPS having absolutely no damn clue where I was at this point, but I had a roadmap spread across the passenger seat. Thankfully, I'd been smart enough to grab one at the last gas station I stopped at when I started to notice civilization becoming scarcer and my cell coverage vanishing.

The road was bumpy and uneven; long gone was anything paved. Woods surround me on all sides, and I swear the deeper I drove up this backroad—if you could even call it that—I actually felt the temperature drop the higher I climbed.

I'd obviously done my research before applying for the job, then more research before accepting the position. He was single, a billionaire in the oil industry, with no children, and wasn't seen much in the social scene. His home—a three-story gargantuan cabin—was half an hour from any kind of civilization. I didn't know if he had others who worked for him to tend to such a large place, but I hoped so. Because there was no way in hell I could even attempt to keep it all clean and organized with just myself.

I came up to a set of massive wrought iron gates. There was a keypad on the driver side of the car, and I rolled my window down to reach out and press the button. I could see the camera pointed directly at me and waited with my heart in my throat as I was granted entrance.

Only a second passed before there was a buzz, and the gates opened, the doors swinging inward. I rolled my window up and squeezed my hands around the steering wheel as I pressed on the gas and made my way up the winding, narrow gravel driveway.

The road seemed to go on forever, but finally there was a break in the trees, and the massive cabin-like estate came into view. It was even more gorgeous than the images online. In fact, I could easily picture it on one of those home and garden elite magazines that showcased rich and famous people's dwellings.

Once my car was in park and the engine off, I sat there a moment and looked out the window. I was nervous, not because of the job, but I'd finally be meeting Finland Hawthorne for the first time. Strangely enough, there hadn't been one clear image of him that I could find on the Internet. They were either blurry and out of focus... or there just weren't any.

So technically, I was going in blind here. Maybe he'd be some scarred and awful man, hater of all things that brought pleasure. Maybe he'd be such a cruel bastard that I'd want to leave as soon as I met him.

How much worse could he be than some of the men I'd come across living in the city?

Well, here goes nothing.

2

Fin

When I placed the ad for a domestic professional online, I hadn't been picky and had little preference and specifications on who I wanted to work for me. As long as they had some kind of experience in the field, respected my privacy, and knew what they were getting into when working for a recluse, I would've given them the job.

But then I'd come across her application, a brutally honest one in the most refreshing way. She had zero experience in this field of work, but was candid about it to the point it should have been deemed unprofessional and an automatic refusal of the job.

But not in my case.

My interest had been instantly piqued to the point I couldn't ignore it. I needed to know more about her, who she was, what she liked. So I researched her, dug up as much information as I could about Catherine Monsieur.

She was a twenty-two-year-old undergrad for Social Science at Clayton Community College.

She still lived with her parents and worked at the local pub... well, up until a couple weeks ago, when she'd given her notice after accepting the position from me. She had no significant other and only surrounded herself with a small circle of close friends.

Her friends and family called her Kitty.

I had taken one look at her picture, and something in me had stirred, awakened. It was like a dormant, primal beast had felt its heart beat for the first time in its life.

It was an unexplainable, all-consuming sensation. I didn't understand it, but I sure as fuck liked it.

And so I hired her on the spot for the simple fact that I wanted to get to know her, wanted her close.

Seeing the picture of her instantly made me want her in the most obscene, filthy ways. I'd never felt such irrefutable desire before. I hadn't been with a woman in so long that I didn't even know how to be tender, how to be soft and caring to the gentler sex. I was a beast, having been called "inhuman" because of my size. When people described me, they said I could snap bones like twigs in my hands.

I'd always kept myself away from others, preferring solitude because my gruff nature tended to turn people off, scared them and had them crossing the street to avoid me. I'd been without any kind of companionship for so long it was now a distant dream. But that had been fine with me. I hadn't needed anyone but myself.

That was... until I'd seen the picture of her, and that had all changed.

But seeing her in the video monitor as she waited at the gate for me to let her in, seeing her in real life—as real as it could be at that moment—something primal and brutal awoke within me.

I sat behind my desk and watched as she drove up the driveway, the security cameras located sporadically around the property giving me every angle possible to watch her. I felt no shame or even guilt at the fact that I watched her every move. And when she pulled up to the front doors and just sat there, staring at the estate, I wondered if I'd scare her away. I did that to plenty of people.

When she climbed out, I felt absolutely zero remorse in how I devoured her body with my gaze. She wore these little cut-off shorts, ones she'd probably end up changing out of sooner rather than later because the air up here was chillier—which was a damn shame. She had legs that were toned and long, and I imagined them wrapped around my waist.

Her T-shirt was thin and white, her bra slightly visible under the light material. And her breasts... fuck, her breasts were high and a perfect handful. My fingers itched to be molded around them.

She had womanly curves, flared hips, and a round, perfect peach-shaped ass.

I sat behind my desk and curled my hands around the wood, my nails digging into the top of it. My cock was rock-hard, and I reached down to adjust the fucker, a harsh groan ripping from me when I touched it. I could've jerked off right now to the sight of her, come so hard that it saturated the front of my slacks.

Fuck, when did I become a dirty bastard?

The moment I first saw her, that's when.

She stopped at the stone steps that lead up to the front porch, tilted her head back, and lifted her hand to shield her eyes from the sun. Her shirt rose up a little bit, a swatch of her creamy, golden skin coming into view. Another animalistic growl left me.

Truth of the matter was, I didn't want her as my fucking cook or housekeeper. I wanted her in my bed, under me, as I plowed between her thighs and made her take every single last inch of me.

I continued to watch her as she walked up the steps. I adjusted the camera view so it was now pointed at her face. Her pixie-like features were delicate, feminine. I found myself lowering my head slightly yet keeping my gaze locked on her image. I felt so fucking... feral.

Her long dark hair brushed the center of her back, and when the wind picked up and blew the tendrils around her cheeks, I felt my heart pound fiercely in my chest. I'd never had this reaction before, never felt fire in my blood, this demon clawing at my gut, wanting to get free, wanting to mount her, to fuck her.

I wanted my mark on her, a testimony to any male who looked in her direction that she was taken. And if they tried to have her, I wanted them to see me and know that with one look I'd tear them limb from limb.

I forced myself to move away from the cameras, stood, adjusted my raging hard-on, and told myself to bring back that aloofness, that disinterest for the human population and I'd be able to get through this initial meeting.

She'd have questions; I was sure plenty of them. I had no doubt she'd done her research on me, had seen the rumors plastered across the Internet. And to be honest, a part of me worried what she thought about me. I'd never given a fuck about anyone's opinion up until now.

And if she tried to delve deeper? Hell, I didn't have an actual backstory to why I was like this. I'd never been a "people person." I always stuck to myself, being an only child with parents who were far too busy with their careers to worry about entertaining their son. But I harbored no ill will toward them, and instead used that time to hone in on skills. I taught myself how to play the piano, learned two languages. I practiced archery, woodworking. I learned the layout of the acreage we owned and studied my father's business so that one day, after he retired, I could run it successfully.

And that day had come five years ago when he and my mother decided to finally retire in the south of France. And after they moved away, I built a house on the hundred acres my family owned for the last three generations.

I exhaled slowly and made my way out of my office, hearing the doorbell ring as soon as I took that first step that would have me descend into the foyer and to the front door.

The closer I got to the door, the more I felt her. I swore I could smell her, could feel her heat, hear her heart beating. I had no doubt she was nervous. I'd seen that anxiousness written on her face on the security monitor as she bit her bottom lip, her straight, little white teeth pulling at the flesh.

I imagined doing that myself, marking her body, putting my claim of ownership all over her.

And then I reached out and opened the door, knowing without even saying an actual word to her, without having seen her in person, that I'd make her mine.

No matter what.

CHAPTER 3

Kitty

The door opened, and I was instantly taken aback by the sheer size of the man standing right inside the entrance.

Finland Hawthorne.

My new employer.

A giant-sized man.

My eyes were level with his lower chest. Yes. His lower chest. He was so tall, so wide and muscular that he was like this statue of rock-solid marble in front of me.

I lifted my gaze up his massive, towering form, my head tilted back, my neck craned so I could look into his face. I'd never in my life felt tinier than I did in this moment. This man was monstrous in size compared to me.

His shoulders were broad, his arms looking so thick I wondered if he could crush bone with little effort. The dark, long-sleeved shirt he wore couldn't hide his muscles; in fact, I was pretty sure they accented them. And his gray slacks covered tree-trunk-sized thighs. He had to be well over six-and-a-half feet tall of solid strength.

The most impure thoughts slammed into my head, ones I shouldn't be thinking about concerning a stranger, but especially about my boss.

I actually felt myself blushing at the lewd image playing on a reel in my mind.

How would it feel to be under him? How much would it hurt to have him inside me? I had absolutely no damn doubt his dick was the size of my forearm, and on that thought—on that image—I broke out in a cold sweat.

I swallowed, my throat tight, realizing we'd just been standing here, me checking him out, Finland Hawthorne obviously noticing that. I was instantly humiliated that our first encounter was him noticing me all but eye-fucking him. And that was a pretty good description of what I'd been doing.

I stared into his eyes, ones that reminded me of

an icy blue tundra. The shade was what I imagined the ocean looked like far north, where it was frigid and barren.

His jaw was cut severely, square, and couldn't be called anything but masculine. Although I could tell he was freshly shaven, he still sported a five o'clock shadow, as if every part of his body refused to fall in line, to follow the rules.

My face was on fire, and I cleared my throat and started rubbing my hands up and down my shorts. It was then I looked down at myself, realizing how unprofessionally dressed I was. I closed my eyes and cursed internally.

I was so unprepared, but what I hadn't been expecting was my employer to be so fucking fine he literally made me speechless.

"Ms. Monsieur, I presume?"

I snapped my head up to look at his face, the sound of his voice slamming right into the most intimate part of my body. And by that, I meant my pussy.

My pussy clenched painfully, the inner muscles aching as if seeking something substantial to grip. Like his cock. Like his dick that I could tell was probably massive.

His voice was deep, so gruff it almost didn't

sound real. I could picture him in some medieval time. Maybe even prehistoric, a caveman, or a Viking wielding an ax, a barbarian about to chop down any foe who stood in his way.

"Mr. Hawthorne?"

He nodded slowly.

He certainly looked like a warrior, a warrior I wanted to be under while he pillaged between my thighs.

Oh my God. I was losing my damn mind for this man.

I noted, realizing several seconds had passed where I hadn't responded. "Yes. That's me." Again, I felt like a fool but straightened my shoulders and continued to look him in the eye. I didn't want to seem like I had absolutely no control over my body, but I had a strong feeling that's exactly how I was portraying myself.

He stepped aside and pulled the door open a little bit more, a silent but universal gesture for me to enter. I stepped over the threshold and could instantly smell him. It was a spicy, woodsy aroma, expensive yet wild and free.

Again, my pussy clenched, and I embarrassingly felt how my panties became damp.

"Do you have bags in the car?"

I froze at the tone of his voice, this demand, yet I had a feeling that was just how he was, how he spoke.

I nodded and licked my lips. He glanced outside at my car then a second later back at me. He held my gaze with his own for an uncomfortable amount of time, as if he could read my thoughts, see the dirty images running through my head.

"I'll get them then show you to your room."

I nodded in response, but he was already outside, striding—stalking—to my car like a sleek panther moving through the jungle.

If this was how I felt upon first meeting him, I didn't know how I'd last or control my libido working for Finland Hawthorne.

3

Fin

I allowed her to ascend the stairs first, not just because I wanted to be a gentleman, but because her ass would be right in my line of sight. Apparently, when it came to this woman, I had zero self-control.

I adjusted my stiff cock as we took the steps, not wanting her to see how I responded physically to her.

As I watched the way the perfect mounds of her bottom moved under her shorts, my cock jerked violently. Every time she lifted her leg to take the next step, I got a tiny peek of that crease where her ass met her thigh. I groaned deeply, thought I'd only done it in my head, but realized the sound had spilled from me deep and low.

I prayed like hell she hadn't heard it, although when I saw the way her hand tightened on the banister, how her step faltered slightly, I knew.

She heard me.

That should've made me feel uncomfortable, made me feel shame, but the truth was, I got this sick satisfaction at the thought of her knowing how much I wanted her.

Once at the top of the stairs, I pointed in the direction for her to go down the hallway. Originally, I had her room set up on the first level. My room was on the second level.

But after I realized how much I wanted her, I knew exactly where she'd be.

In the room right next to mine... and eventually in my bed.

"This one," I grumbled, pissed that I couldn't control myself. Never in my life had I been unable to stifle my emotions or keep the apathetic emotions at the forefront.

But Kitty was an anomaly, one I wanted to delve deeper into.

I meant that literally and figuratively.

She stopped by the polished double oak doors

and moved to the side to allow me to open them. I knew it was because she was nervous. She kept twisting her hands together in front of her, kept biting her lower lip anxiously.

I set her two bags down and saw the way she looked at me from under her lashes. I'd been surprised to see only the two bags. I assumed being relocated she'd have packed enough to fully move in.

I stepped close, my body only an inch from hers, and reached out to turn the handle. I kept my eyes locked on hers the whole time. My teeth were locked tight as I inhaled the sweetness that came from her.

Then I pushed the door open but didn't move. "This is your room," I said, my voice serrated. I should have moved aside to give her more space. It was a bastardly thing to do to crowd her, but I wanted her to brush up against me when she stepped inside.

And she did.

It was only the slightest of brushes, but it was there nonetheless.

It took a hell of a lot of control not to grab her nape, pull her to my chest, and lean down to claim her mouth.

"Thank you, Mr. Hawthorne."

It was like the very sound of her voice, the way my name rolled off her tongue, held a thousand bolts of electricity. It traveled through my entire body, lighting me up.

"Call me Fin. Or Finland. Mr. Hawthorne was my father." I shouldn't have said that. I should have at least tried to keep things semi-professional, even if I felt like they were anything but in my case.

But shit, I wanted her to say my name all damn day. It made me harder just knowing it slid between *her* lips.

I had to keep reminding myself I needed to act like I had my shit under control, be professional, and pretend I didn't want to press her up against the wall and fuck the hell out of her.

I stifled the low growl that would've spilled from my mouth again and followed her into the room. No one had ever used it. In fact, no one had ever used any of these rooms on the upper floor.

I wanted Kitty close. It was an undeniable need. There was no point in even trying to fight. I didn't want to.

She glanced around, and I could see surprise written on her expression. She was shocked by her surroundings. The room was lavish, and although I had nobody to spoil, no wife or children, no significant other that I could spend my money on, that didn't mean I didn't enjoy the fruits of my labor.

So I built this extravagant home for just myself, decorated the rooms with high-end items, expensive decor. The works.

I spent my money on other items, other things. Charities, built organizations for victims of domestic violence, donated to food banks to feed the hungry. But even after spending my money on all these things, I still had deep pockets. So deep they were black fucking holes.

The very thought of dying and not having anyone to carry on my legacy, no descendants to leave any of this fortune to, had never made me feel depressed until right now, until I looked at Kitty and wondered if she'd be mine.

And if she would never be mine....

No, I wouldn't even entertain that thought. I would claim her. It was an easy decision.

As easy as breathing.

4

Kitty

Mr. Hawthorne—Fin, as he asked me to call him—left me half an hour ago. He'd told me to get situated and comfortable, to "make myself at home."

I'd unpacked, put my clothes in the dresser, and now just sat on the edge of the bed looking around. I was a little uncomfortable, if I were being honest. This room certainly didn't feel like a place a member of the staff would stay. It was lavish, extravagant. It was opulent.

The four-poster bed was lush and massive, the mattress like a cloud. The pictures on the walls showed close-ups of flowers, silky-smooth leaves, bright pops of color.

I idly wondered if Fin had taken the pictures. They looked professional, but very personal, intimate too.

Tonight, we'd be discussing my responsibilities, but first he told me we'd be dining together. He said after I was settled, I was to come downstairs, that he had the local caterer deliver dinner.

It was just dinner.

Yet it felt like so much *more* for some reason.

I changed out of my cut-off shorts and T-shirt, feeling that I was too exposed, too unprofessional. Instead, I slipped on a black dress, the hem falling to my knees. There was a white Peter Pan collar at my throat. And the sleeves were these cute little capped ones. Not too much skin showing and hopefully made me look like he hadn't made a mistake hiring me, that he wouldn't regret it.

I was nervous. And I had no idea why. No, that was a lie, a fabrication I told myself to try to make this easier. Because as soon as I'd seen Finland Hawthorne standing on the other side of that front door, something in me shifted. I felt the world tilt under my feet, the air become thinner, the temperature rising.

He had this raw animal magnetism to him, and it was so potent, so powerful that it gripped its claws into my body and refused to let go. And I didn't want it to release me. I wanted it to pull me in, to consume me, to take the world and reality away and just let me live in this fantasy.

I walked over to the bedroom door but stopped before opening it. I closed my eyes and just breathed in and out for several long moments, willing my heart to slow, my pulse to be steady. I could do this, keep things strictly work related, keep my emotions in check.

But I'd never felt this kind of connection to someone before, and certainly never imagined having it with a virtual stranger.

And the way he looked at me, those piercing blue eyes that seemed to stare right into my soul, made me feel that maybe this wasn't one-sided.

I opened my eyes and cleared my throat, straightening my shoulders and reaching for the knob all simultaneously.

I made my way out of the room and down the stairs, heading into first the kitchen, seeing it was empty, and then wandering around for a moment before I found the dining room. I noticed the table first. It was long, polished, and ornate. The edges were raw, giving it a rustic look, but the top was glossy, giving it a classy appearance.

The table was already set, the food under silver trays and platters. I wondered if Fin had done it. He didn't seem like the type of man to do domestic things, yet I really knew nothing about him aside from the generic business side of Finland Hawthorne that I found online.

I didn't see the man in question and just stood there, not knowing if I should take a seat or wait for him to show.

Only a minute passed before I felt him. He stood right behind me, his very presence rocking me to the core. My awareness was heightened, every erogenous zone coming alive.

I felt the heat from him slamming into my back and actually forcing me to close my eyes.

"Ms. Monsieur," he said in that deliciously deep voice of his.

"Kitty," I said before I could stop myself. "Please, call me Kitty."

He moved around me then, and I told myself not to shiver as his shoulder brushed against me, to keep myself level. It was hard. So damn hard.

My head didn't even reach his shoulders, and I

curled my hands into tight fists at my sides as feminine appreciation washed through me at that fact.

He walked up to the table, gripped the back of one of the chairs, and pulled it out. Then he just stood there and stared at me, this unspoken demand for me to take a seat.

I licked my lips and took that first step, each one after becoming harder for some reason. And when I finally sat down, I felt him push the chair in a little bit more. I felt him so close to me, and I swore I heard him inhale close to my ear, as if he were taking in my very essence.

I couldn't breathe as I watched him walk around to the other side of the table, taking his seat across from me. He seemed worlds away, and after a second, it was as if he realized that too, because he let out a rough grumble before taking his place setting and standing.

He walked back over to me, and I felt my eyes widen when he took the seat right beside mine. The air became hotter, thicker, the room feeling like it was closing in on me. Then he just stared at me again. I felt so on edge, so bared to this man despite being fully dressed, even though we hadn't said more than a few words.

"You're not hungry?" he asked in that deep rumble that did wicked things to my body.

I clenched my thighs under the table, trying to calm myself. I had my hands in my lap, thankful the table blocked his view from how I dug my nails against my thighs.

Why did he make me feel so damn unsteady?

"I am, thank you." I glanced at my plate then for the first time since sitting down.

There was a piece of steak—which looked juicy and thick and cooked to perfection. Mashed potatoes with gravy, a buttered roll, and green beans that were all perfectly arranged on the porcelain plate.

A side salad was beside the plate, and a small olive oil and vinegar carafe for the dressing was next to it. There was a glass of water to my left, and a glass of red wine to my right. There were so many pieces of silverware that I had no idea which fork I was supposed to use.

"Eat and then we can discuss business matters."

For being such a larger than life mountain man, Fin spoke eloquently, as if he'd been running boardrooms all his life. I supposed he had, and so I listened to him, picked up one of the forks, and started eating the food that was so good I actually had to hold in a moan of pleasure.

The steak was tender and juicy, the mashed potatoes buttery with a hint of garlic. The green beans
had the perfect amount of crisp to them when I took
a bite.

There was no rush as we ate, and I was surprised
by the small talk he initiated, and even more
shocked that it was comfortable and not at all forced.
I found myself really enjoying this time with him.

He cleared our plates once we were finished and
left for only a moment before returning, a plate in
each of his hands. He set the dessert down in front of
me, the cake looking decadent and moist.

"I hope you enjoy lemon raspberry cake. I get it
frequently from Tosco's, the little bakery in town. It's
called something fancy, but nothing I can ever
pronounce accurately."

I smiled and it was genuine.

That first bite had me actually moaning, the cake
sweet but not overboard. It was rich but not too
much so. It was thick and soft, spongy, and the raspberry sauce tasted so fresh it was like I'd picked the
raspberries myself just this morning.

I was almost halfway finished with the cake
when I felt Fin watching me. I snapped my attention
to him, saw his eyes locked on mine, and swallowed
the cake I had in my mouth almost roughly.

His expression... it was primal.

He watched me with his head lowered and his eyes seeming to glow with something that I couldn't quite place, but also something that had my entire body coming alive all over again. It was a look that said one thing.

I like what I see.

I don't know how I knew that, but it was so loud it was as if he roared it to me, demanding I admit that I was his.

I'm losing my damn mind, projecting what I feel and want onto this man.

Once we were finished with dessert, he took those plates as well and then refilled my wine glass. I was already feeling a little lightheaded, unused to drinking alcohol despite having worked at a pub back in the city. This was my second full glass, and I couldn't help but feel more at ease, relaxed, drinking the liquid courage.

So I took another hearty drink and then set the glass back down, keeping my fingers around the stem, letting the pads move along the smooth crystal.

"I'm an easy man to work with," he finally said.

I snapped my gaze in his direction, not realizing I'd been focused on my hand as my fingers played along the bottom of the glass. "What?" I prompted softly.

"I'm gruff, like things a certain way, but aside from that, I won't be in your way."

How wrong was it that I *wanted* him to be in my way?

I couldn't help but feel that he didn't quite mean that last part. It was the pitch of his voice, how low and deep it was, the way he flicked his eyes in my direction as if daring me to listen to the underlying message.

"I read through the contract fully, if that's what you're worried about?" I grabbed the napkin and wiped my mouth. "I assure you I won't let you down, Mr. Haw—"

"Fin. Call me Fin." He said that so... demandingly. He cleared his throat and shifted slightly on the chair. "You're welcome to make up your own times, and you're not required to do all those duties."

"But the contract—"

"It's standard. A formality. I make the rules."

A shiver of... something so dark and demanding, so potent, raced through me.

"I don't expect for you to tend to the entire house alone. I have a professional service come in once a month to deep clean." He stared at me right in the eyes.

I nodded, thankful he pointed out that I wouldn't be responsible for this gargantuan house.

"You're able to prepare meals daily?"

I nodded again. "Of course."

"Light cleaning would be essential. I don't go in many of the rooms, so it would be nice to have those checked to make sure things aren't getting... stale."

"Of course," I repeated.

For the next twenty minutes, we continued talking about what he expected me to do. Although he said I could make up my own times, that two days of the week would be for me to do with as I please, I knew I'd be strict with how I conducted myself here.

I had to be, or I'd unravel in the presence of sin, and Fin was full-on sin.

I could already feel myself doing that now, the tendrils of want and desire mixing with each other to create this combustible flame inside me.

He discussed finances, money being deposited into my account biweekly, and how I'd have a "company car," and a weekly household allowance to purchase groceries and other supplies I needed. He wasn't picky about meals either, but I made note of what he liked and didn't like and knew I'd have things planned out a week in advance.

I also reminded myself to get that lemon raspberry cake a couple times a week. I'd seen how much he enjoyed it.

A part of me wanted to make life easier for myself here by being organized, but I also wanted to show him that I could handle this, that he wouldn't regret hiring me. Although I had no experience in any of this, I would take my job seriously and be proud of it.

Once we were finished talking, he asked if I wanted another glass of wine. It was tempting, but I knew if I had any more, I'd wake up with a headache. So I declined, excused myself for the night, and I made my way back toward my room.

I found myself taking a detour though. I found the study, or maybe it was his office. I saw the library, the shelving from ceiling to floor. The walls seemed to be built specifically to hold books. If I'd been an avid reader, I would've been in heaven at that moment, but even I could appreciate the beauty of all the leather bound titles.

I made my way back upstairs to go to my room for the night, since I wanted to be up relatively early. I had a lot to do tomorrow, not because there were tasks given to me right off the bat, but because I wanted to be fully prepared for my new position.

When I reached the top of the stairs, I made my way toward my room. Most of the doors on either side of me were closed, but when I neared the one that was directly beside mine, I couldn't help but slow when I saw it was partially opened.

The scent coming out of it was purely male and all Fin. I knew without having to ask that this was his room. Knowing he'd sleep right beside my room had this weird feeling settling in my belly.

The door was open enough that I could see the massive bed across the room, almost identical to mine, but twice the size, and that was saying something, since mine wasn't anything to scoff about. Then again, a man of Fin's size and stature would need a monstrous bed.

The dirty thoughts that slammed into my head had my cheeks instantly feeling hot. They were images of me naked, of him above me, the sheets a tangled mess around us, sweat pouring off our bodies because we'd been going at it all night like animals.

Oh my God. Get yourself under control.

I forced myself to move away and head to my room. Once inside, I shut the door and leaned against it. And then I just inhaled and exhaled until I felt my pulse start to steady, until I felt like I was steady enough on my own two feet.

I had no idea how I was going to survive being Finland Hawthorne's employee, because after only being here for this short time, I already felt like a big fucking mess where he was concerned.

5

Fin

I'd jerked off twice since I said goodnight to Kitty, and it hadn't helped. In fact, it had made my arousal even stronger, more potent.

I'd never felt anything like this before. It was like this fire burning me alive, and the accelerant was Kitty.

I should've probably felt like a dirty bastard thinking these lower, obscene thoughts concerning her. But I didn't. And I refused to stop thinking about her.

This was her first day, she hadn't even been here twenty-four hours, but I'd already deemed her as mine.

I'd claim her, show her that no one else would have her but me. It was an insane thought, a crazy feeling to have, but it was as real as the air I was drawing into my lungs. It was as solid as the heart beating in my chest.

I couldn't let her go. I wouldn't. That wasn't even plausible to me.

But I was a patient man. I could wait until she was ready, until she felt what I felt, until she needed me with such a burning intensity it consumed her from the tips of her toes to the top of her head.

I'd watch her, touch myself as I thought about her, and all the while my feelings, my need and obsession for her, would grow.

When I wanted something, I did whatever it took to make it mine.

And I'd never wanted anything more than Kitty.

6

Kitty

I'd been lying in bed for the last twenty minutes, unable to sleep, because my mind and body were running feral.

I breathed out in annoyance with myself and shifted onto my back, staring above. The lights from the patio came through the partially opened curtains and washed across the ceiling. I didn't know what it was about Fin, but he set me on edge. But he also started this fire in me. He had me wanting more... more than I ever thought even possible.

But I wasn't stupid. I knew realistically we'd never be together. He was my boss and was so socially withdrawn that he probably didn't want a relationship at all. Not friendly, and certainly not romantic.

So the fantasies playing in my head would have to do, but if they controlled me this much, how could I even concentrate to do my job, to think rationally, act normally in his presence as time passed?

I pushed the covers off me and sat up, swinging my body to the left so my legs were hanging off the edge of the mattress. The frame was so high off the ground that my feet didn't even touch the wood floor.

I slid off the bed, the soles of my feet coming in contact with the coldness, and padded over to the window, pulling the curtain aside and looking out. This room had a small balcony that overlooked the backyard, if it even could be called the latter. The natural wilderness surrounded the home, and the only thing I could see were thick trees as far as the eye could see. Below, there was a hot tub that sat on the massive deck that came off the living room patio doors. I'd seen it briefly when I wandered around, finding the dining room.

I rose on my toes slightly to look over the banister, my vantage point not giving me much of a good view, but I could see the lid was open on the hot tub, and the water was bubbling from the jets.

I was about to turn around and head back to bed, try to get some sleep, since I had to wake up so early to start the day, but a big shadow heading toward the hot tub had me stilling. And then I saw him, Fin wearing a thick white robe, standing on the other side of the spa, looking at the water. It was late, and I was surprised to see him still up, although maybe he couldn't sleep, the same as me.

My heart instantly started racing just at the mere sight of him, but then he went for the tie at the side of the robe, undid it, and pushed the material off his shoulders.

I'd known he was heavily muscular just by the way he filled out his clothes. I could see the definition under the material. But I wasn't prepared to see all that flash in the... well, flesh.

And he definitely had a lot of it: tan, hard, and undeniably masculine flesh.

And his nakedness. Good God, it was like he'd been created with the sole purpose to please a woman, like whoever created him wanted Fin to make a woman scream and have her walking bowlegged the next day.

My gaze immediately went to the area between his thighs, as if there were a magnet leading me there. I actually felt my eyes widen as I stared at what he sported. He wasn't even hard, yet his damn dick was so big that the very first thought I had in my head was that his cock couldn't possibly fit inside any woman comfortably.

My tongue felt too big for the inside of my mouth, and my heart was beating so fast it was painful. I actually placed a hand on my chest, as if that could still the rapid beat, as if that could somehow calm it.

Not only was I having a hard-enough time gathering my composure when Fin was fully fucking clothed, but now that I'd seen him naked... yeah, good luck with reminding myself that he was my new boss.

I should've turned away, but for long moments, I stayed there, watching as he slipped into the hot tub, taking note of the way his muscles bunched and moved like a stealthy animal. He leaned back against the side, his arms stretched out on either side and hanging over the edge.

I couldn't see his face any longer, but I didn't need to. His image, the very visage of him, would be ingrained in my head for the rest of my life.

I forced myself to move away then, went back to bed, slipped under the covers, and knew that come morning I would be tired as hell. Sleep didn't even seem plausible right now.

And as I lay on my back and stared at the ceiling, my hand slid along my belly, between my thighs, and under the edge of my panties.

It was after I touched myself, made myself come so hard I saw stars, that I finally fell asleep.

And I knew I'd dream about Fin. I anticipated it.

7

Fin

I knew she'd been watching me last night when I'd gotten into the hot tub naked. I'd felt her eyes on me, as if she were touching my body, stroking me. Thankfully, I'd been in the water just as I started getting hard. That wasn't something I wanted her to see... not yet anyway.

I'd gotten up before the sun had risen this morning, knowing I needed to get some work done before Kitty consumed my thoughts, and my focus the rest of the day was shot.

I'd heard her rise about six in the morning, and because I couldn't control myself where she was concerned, I turned on all the cameras in the house just so I could see her while I worked.

Security was important to me, not just because of personal preference, but because of who I was. Having power meant you had enemies, people who wanted to take what was yours. All the security cameras might be overkill, but I was a firm believer in being safe rather than being sorry. And right now, I'd never been happier to have them in the house than I was now.

Aside from the bathrooms and the bedrooms, there were cameras in every other room and placed around the exterior of the property. And right now, I watched her sit at the dining room table with a cup of coffee in front of her, and a notebook beside that.

She had one leg bent up, the foot resting on the bottom of the chair. The sun came through the window and had this glow all around her.

She looked beautiful.

Kitty kept running her fingers around her knee as she wrote in the book. I zoomed in on the image of her and watched as she bit her bottom lip, tugging at that pink flesh, making it redder, slightly swollen from the subtle abuse.

Her long dark hair was pulled up into a ponytail, little wisps having fallen out around the crown, teasing her temples. I wanted to run my fingers around those tendrils, see if they were as soft as they looked.

I felt my hands curl against the edge of the table, and it was when I heard my nails digging into the wood that I loosened my grip. This woman had so much power over me that I didn't even recognize myself.

Here I was watching someone without their knowledge, essentially stalking them, was obsessed with them... already fucking claiming them, and they didn't even know it.

Who was this man I'd become?

I cleared my throat and turned away from the cameras, running a hand over my jaw, feeling the scruff underneath. I hadn't even bothered shaving this morning. She consumed my thoughts to the point that I couldn't even focus on anything else.

What I did know for certain was that I wouldn't be able to concentrate until I had her as mine. But even then, I knew once I tasted her, knew how she felt, how wet she'd become for me, I'd be so addicted nothing else would matter but her.

Nothing would ever come close to Kitty.

Hell, that's how it was going now, and I hadn't even claimed her fully.

I stood and left my study, heading into the kitchen to pour myself a big cup of coffee. I had Tosco deliver pastries first thing this morning, another thing I indulged in quite frequently.

But when you lived alone, picking up certain habits that comforted and placated you seemed to be the norm in my case.

I stepped into the kitchen and saw the pastry box on the counter. I opened it up and saw she hadn't taken one, but then again, I'd only seen that cup of coffee in front of her when I watched her.

She needed to eat. *I want to feed her.* That thought slammed into my head so strongly I knew I would do just that once she was mine.

I put a danish on a small plate, grabbed one for me, and balanced it in my mouth as I took the coffee mug. I made my way back to where Kitty was and set the plate in front of her. She'd been so immersed in writing in her notebook that she didn't even realize I was there until I was right beside her.

"Oh. Good morning," she said and smiled, and it lit up the entire fucking room.

It fucking lit me up.

She glanced at the plate. "Thank you." The way she said it had this little mewling tone laced in it, and I clenched my jaw to hold in my pleasured groan.

I took the seat across from her and brought my mug to my lips, taking a long drink. I took note of her coffee. It was milky, maybe more cream than actual coffee. I bet it was sweet too. I made a mental note for future reference so I could make it for her in the mornings.

I noticed the morning paper sitting on the table and reached for it, unfolding it and turning to the business section. I scanned the pages, but I kept finding myself looking up at her.

She sat the same way, her foot braced on the edge of the chair as she wrote in her notebook. She was picking at the danish, breaking off little pieces and bringing it to her mouth, and then licking off the glaze that was on the tips of those digits.

I felt that powerful yet familiar arousal start at the base of my spine as I watched her little pink tongue move out and drag across her skin. It was so innocent, yet so extremely sexual in the same breath.

My traitorous cock started to harden, and I cleared my throat a little too gruffly. She looked up at me, and I quickly looked down at the paper, feigning interest in the stock market. After a few moments of silence, both of us enjoying our coffee, she pushed her notebook toward me, and I glanced up at her.

"I've made out a menu for the week. If you want to look over it and let me know if there's anything you dislike or would like me to change, I can make note for future meals and adjust this one."

I looked down at what she'd written. She was meticulous, organized as she broke down lunch and dinner, even breakfast, although I told her I rarely ate breakfast during the week because I was up so early. But to be honest, I would've eaten anything she put in front of me any time of the day. As long as she was the one who prepared it, I would've gotten satisfaction from anything.

"It all looks wonderful," I said and meant it. She beamed, was actually happy by my response, which in turn pleased me to no end.

She took back the notebook and gave me a short nod before rising. "Great. I made the menu this week with the ingredients we have here at the house. I'll probably have to make a grocery run next week, if that's okay?"

"Anything you want or need, it's yours." And I meant that in more ways than one.

She looked away quickly, and I didn't miss how

her cheeks started to turn pink. Had I embarrassed her? Maybe her thoughts were just as dirty as mine.

I wanted to place my hand on her face and see if her skin was warm from the blush. When she cleared her throat and glanced back at me, I was snapped out of my fantasies. She let me know where she'd be if I needed anything then made her way out.

I sat there and just watched her walk away, my focus on her ass, my control barely hanging on. I had no fucking clue how I'd go slow with her, how I'd restrain myself from clearing the table every morning and fucking her on it.

Hell, I could fuck her three times a day and it still wouldn't be enough.

She woke up this beast in me, and for the first time in my life, I was actually worried that I'd have no self-control.

8

Kitty

A week later

I didn't know how to accurately describe my work environment with Fin, and I didn't know if it was just because of how I felt for him, this burning desire I had, but every time he was near—which, if I were being honest, was constant—I felt this electrifying intensity.

And he did seem to always be around.

Watching me, tracking me with his eyes, his focus on me so intense I felt as if he reached out and smoothed his fingers along my cheek.

Maybe in any other circumstance I would've felt uncomfortable, that it would've been inappropriate.

But because of what I felt for Fin, how I liked his eyes on me, like this silent claim I sensed every time he was near, I let myself indulge in these emotions.

I pushed all those thoughts out of my head and finished buying the supplies for dinner tonight. This was the first time I'd ventured out of the house and off the property. I'd taken one of his cars—the big-ass SUV he insisted I use—and explored the town.

It was quaint, but the businesses were well-known, not just with the residents but in the state as well. I'd researched them before moving here. For such a small town, it held many successful companies, places I knew would have boomed and flourished in the city.

But the company that was the most successful was definitely Hawthorne Oil. The company covered the tri-state area, and probably even farther than that. Once all the technological lingo started popping up as I researched, it all became lost on me.

I pushed my cart up to one of the empty registers and started unloading the items on the belt, mentally checking off everything on my grocery list to make sure I got everything. I was going to make lasagna from scratch, the one thing my mom had shown me how to cook on many occasions. It was probably the only thing that I didn't burn half the time. Strangely enough, I hadn't been ruining the meals here. Maybe it was because I tried to please him, that I wanted to see that pleasure on his face as he ate the food I prepared just for him.

I was a tangled mess of need and want inside.

I was going to stop by Tosco's and pick up a lemon raspberry cake for dinner tonight. I actually felt my cheeks heat as I thought about the way Fin watched me the last time I'd eaten the cake. His eyes had been locked on my mouth as I'd taken in each forkful, and although I felt extremely on edge, as if I were a specimen under a microscope, I couldn't lie and say I didn't like him looking at me.

There was this very animalistic aura that surrounded him. It made me feel feminine in every single way.

I cleared my throat as my thoughts tried to go down a much dirtier path. I wished in these instances that I had girlfriends I could talk to, people I could share these intimate details with, but I'd always been what people called antisocial. I was just a shy girl, an introvert. Maybe that's why this job had called to me so much.

Here I was out in the middle of nowhere, the wilderness surrounding me, only one person to interact with. And even going into town was small and intimate, nothing like the city where it felt congested and like I was suffocating. *I could live here for the rest of my life,* I thought.

Once I paid and had all the bagged groceries back in the cart, I made my way out of the grocery store and toward the SUV. I stopped before I got to the street to make sure no cars were coming, and my focus landed on a young guy leaning against the side of the store. He had one foot braced on the brick, a cigarette hanging from his lips. His other hand held a bottle wrapped in a brown paper bag. You didn't have to be a rocket scientist to know what was in it.

He pulled the cigarette out of his mouth and exhaled a cloud of smoke before bringing that paper bag wrapped bottle to his mouth and taking a long drink. And the entire time, his focus was on me. He couldn't be much more than my age, maybe a year or two older than I was, but he definitely had this aged look, like he'd seen a lot of shit in his short years.

He looked rough around the edges, as if he spent more time on the streets than at home. His clothes were disheveled and a day away from being utterly filthy. I noticed the serpent tattoo on his arm, one that looked like it had been given to him in the dark with how badly it was done.

His eyes were locked on me, the expression he

wore, the way he slowly smiled when he pulled the bottle away, showing a missing tooth at the side of his mouth, had my body revolting.

I made my way across the street and quickly went toward the SUV. I didn't like the way he made me feel. It was the way some men made me feel when I had to walk home from the pub a few nights.

Dirty.

They made me feel lewd and obscene, as if I were naked, and nothing I could do could shield myself from them.

Once the back door was open, I started shoving in the grocery bags, just wanting to get in the vehicle, wanting to get back to the house... back to Fin. That last bit didn't surprise me, although it should. I liked his presence.

He made me feel safe, not just because he was a big, Viking-sized man, but because there was a presence about him that made me feel like nothing could penetrate the safety that surrounded me when I was with him.

I put the last bag in the back and shut the door and was about to turn around and put the cart in the little corral, when a shocked gasp left me. The guy who'd been standing by the side of the building was now on the other side of the cart, his hand on the red handle, his cigarette now gone as he grinned at me.

He brought the bottle up and took another drink before saying, "You have a couple dollars you could spare?" His voice was scratchy, as if he'd been smoking for the past forty years, although he hadn't even been alive that long.

He gave me a wider grin. I swallowed but didn't answer right away. It wasn't like I wasn't used to people asking for money. That happened quite frequently in the city. But I just felt uncomfortable with this man, as if what he really wanted had nothing to do with cash.

I slowly shook my head. "I'm sorry. I don't." His smile faded, and he moved around the cart, coming closer to me. I shifted the cart so it was still between us.

"You're telling me all those groceries you just bought, this big, nice SUV you drive, you can't spare a couple bucks to someone in need?"

I started to get really nervous. "This is my employer's vehicle. I'm sorry. I can't help you." I started pushing the cart toward the corral, but when he gripped my forearm and jerked me back, instinct took over.

His grip was strong, bruising even, and I knew

he'd be going for my purse next. After that? I didn't know. He seemed desperate for just about anything if he was willing to attack someone in the parking lot of a grocery store while it was still light out.

But living in the city meant you had to know how to take care of yourself. It had been something my father instilled in me when I was younger. So I'd taken self-defense classes religiously. I'd never had to use them, not until now.

I brought my knee up right to his groin, and the grunt of pain that came from him gave me pride. He doubled over, grabbing his crotch as he struggled to catch his breath.

He stumbled backward, his body hitting one of the other vehicles, the car alarm going off and the brown-paper-covered liquor bottle falling from his grasp. The bottle didn't break, but the sound of it clanking on the pavement seemed to echo loudly. The alcohol that was left inside poured out onto the asphalt.

He hauled ass out of there, the commotion drawing attention. I shoved the cart in the corral and got in the Suburban quickly, locking the doors and squeezing the steering wheel tightly.

My heart was beating like a racehorse, and a light sheen of sweat covered my body. I looked down at my forearm, the skin red and feeling raw. I knew there would be a bruise before the night was over with.

Half an hour later, I pulled in front of the house and cut the engine. My pulse had calmed slightly, but my mind was still running wild over the situation. My arm burned, the redness starting to show purple and blue on my skin.

I closed my eyes and just breathed. I pushed the experience away—tried to, at least—knowing I couldn't let it affect me or I'd obsess over it. Things could have gone a lot worse, but they didn't. I'd handled myself, diffused the situation just like I'd been taught, and I was whole.

Maybe I should have called the police, but I'd just wanted to get out of there. And besides, it wasn't like I knew who the guy was. Aside from the serpent tattoo on his arm and the missing tooth he sported, he was probably like any other guy who thought they could take advantage.

I exhaled once more and smoothed my hands over my thighs. Things weren't so bad, I kept telling myself. I let my mind go to Fin and it made me feel more at ease.

He made me feel more at ease.

The one thing about Finland Hawthorne was he

not only wanted meals prepared each night, but he wanted me to actually eat those meals with him. At first, I declined, not feeling comfortable. I was his employee, after all, and eating with my boss seemed very personal and almost intimate.

But he insisted, almost demanded, and after the first couple times of my initial awkwardness, I started looking forward to these moments where we sat across from each other and just talked. He was a quiet man, reserved, very personal. And that's how it had always been with him.

But I felt like he opened up to me, little by little, piece by piece. He wanted to know so much about me... the little things, what I liked and disliked, what my favorite season was, if I preferred horror or comedy movies. And telling him about me was so easy. I wanted to share bits of myself with the man I was falling for harder each day.

It was dangerous to feel these things, and a part of me wished I could stop.

I actually felt myself smile as I thought of those things, how he made me feel. Thinking about him pushed away the horrible experience at the grocery store. I inhaled, just letting it sink in, just letting myself absorb it.

I'd have to face these feelings eventually. I

couldn't keep pushing them down, couldn't keep hiding them. And although eventually I'd have to be honest with him, because it would just be too hard working for Fin while my feelings for him continued to grow, a part of me thought that maybe this wasn't one-sided.

The way he looked at me constantly, as if he always had to know where I was, certainly wasn't something an employer did. Not that I experienced anyway.

So maybe if I was honest, he'd be honest as well?

Or maybe if I told him the truth, I'd lose my job, have to go back into the city, and I'd never feel this way for another person again.

9

Fin

If I were being honest, Kitty leaving the house set me on edge. I didn't like her away from me, and I didn't want to scare her off by being overly possessive. But when she told me she was going to the store to get groceries for the week, I nearly told her I'd take her.

Don't smother her.

Don't scare her off.

That's what I told myself over and over again, and I'd been surprised as hell at myself that I actually listened to that inner voice. I hadn't wanted to, that was for damn sure, but I let her go, watched her take my Suburban, insisting she use that vehicle because it was the safest, because it was big like a fucking tank.

And when an hour passed, then nearly two hours, I started to pace, feeling like a trapped tiger. *The town is a good half hour away*, I kept telling myself. It would take time to get there, for her to shop, for her to come back.

I needed to quit being an obsessive, crazy asshole. But thinking these things, feeling this way for Kitty, came naturally, so naturally it should terrify me.

But it didn't.

I tried to focus on work while she'd been gone, but I realized that not having her in the house, not knowing she was near and safe, made it impossible.

There was an alert from the security system that let me know a vehicle was at the gate. I looked at the monitor and saw the SUV, actually breathing out in relief. I felt like this weight lifted off my chest, knowing she was finally back.

Once she pulled the vehicle to a stop in front of the house, I was out of my seat and heading outside. I opened the front door and made my way down the steps just as she was getting out of the driver side. She popped the back of the vehicle, and I went around to start grabbing bags.

"You don't have to help," she said softly, and I waved off her comment.

Of course I was going to help. What kind of man would I be if I made her do this shit on her own?

It took about five minutes to get all the groceries in the house. I noticed she was avoiding me, not looking at me, keeping her distance. It didn't sit well with me and had my hackles rising. I followed her into the kitchen and studied her face. She looked nervous as she continued to bite her bottom lip, pulling at the pink flesh.

"Is everything okay?" The first thing that came to mind, that had every protective instinct rising in me, was something happened in town. She seemed fine before she left, but now? Now, she looked—acted— almost on edge.

She nodded and said, "I'm fine."

I was successful in what I did, not only because I knew how to run a multimillion-dollar company, but because I also knew how to read people. I knew when they were lying, knew when they were nervous. And there was definitely something wrong with Kitty. I was also successful at what I did, because I didn't allow a challenge to go unchecked. And if I wanted something— the truth—I didn't stop until it was mine, until I uncovered it, until I knew all its secrets.

I leaned against the entryway frame of the kitchen, crossing my arms over my chest and just watched her. She started unloading the groceries and setting them on the counters, but I took note that she kept favoring one side toward me.

She was hiding something.

I moved farther into the kitchen so I could look directly at her, so she couldn't avoid me. And then I examined her, trying to look for signs on what was wrong. She kept lifting her eyes to me and darting them away.

"I feel like something's wrong, Kitty. What happened in town?"

She smiled and shook her head. "I just drove around for a little bit to get the layout of town then went to the grocery store."

I let my gaze travel over her face, along her neck and shoulders, looked at one arm, then went lower still. I was about to continue my way down to see where she was injured, but the mark on her arm had my entire body tightening instantly.

The skin was red, with undertones of purple and blue underneath. A fucking bruise. The mark normally wouldn't have had me on edge for the most part, but it was the fact that it was very clearly an indentation of fingers.

I braced my hands on the granite island in the kitchen and leaned forward, my gaze still locked on her wrist. "What happened?" I tried to ease my tone. The last thing I wanted to do was frighten her. "Who did that to you?" I felt enraged.

Somebody touched her.

Somebody hurt her.

She exhaled as if tired and placed her hands flat on the counter before looking up at me. She wasn't afraid of me, of my tone. I sensed that from her. Good.

I tried to be gentle, to be soft with her, but I was the type of man who was anything but. But I'd try, I'd try really fucking hard for her, because she deserved that and more.

I stared into her eyes, wanting to tell her that I could be that safe space she needed, that I'd protect her, keep her safe. I could see that resistance fade on keeping whatever she was hiding to herself. She sighed once more and looked down at her hands that were still braced on the counter.

"It was just some guy at the grocery store. I'm sure he was drunk. I could smell the alcohol pouring off of him."

Although outwardly I probably looked like her words hadn't affected me, but the truth was, they did. My blood was boiling, everything inside me demanding I go find this fucker and rearrange his face.

"He put his hands on you?" I felt pretty good for not sounding like a deranged animal as I said that. She nodded slowly and started gently rubbing at her bruised wrist. "Do you know who he was?" My heart was beating a mile a minute.

"No," she said and shook her head.

"Did he have any distinguishing features?" I tried to sound curious, nonchalant, but I heard the hardness creeping in my voice.

She looked at me for a long moment before saying, "I'm fine, Fin. I promise."

"Kitty," I said and leaned in a little closer. "Did he have any marks? Scars? Tattoos? Anything like that?" The town was small enough, and I'd lived here my whole life, so unless he just moved here, I'd know who this fucker was.

Her throat worked as she swallowed. "He had a snake tattoo on his arm. And he was missing a tooth."

I growled low, let that fucking sound leave me

with so much power I saw her eyes widen from the fact.

Josh.

I knew who the bastard was. He was a town drunk, a lowlife who harassed anyone who wasn't a local. He'd been arrested for petty shit more times than anyone could count. And because Kitty had just moved here, he probably assumed she was just passing through or too brand new to know what a piece of shit he was.

I was going to beat that fucker's ass.

"That look on your face," she said softly, and I forced my grip on the counter to relax.

I pulled back my shoulders and straightened, giving her a smile, but I felt as if it didn't reach my eyes. "What look?"

I saw her swallow again, and then she was rubbing her palms up and down her thighs. "It's a look like you want to go find him."

That's because I do. I will find him.

I gave her another smile, this one pulling at the corner of my mouth. "Go after him?" I tried to appear like I was relaxed when I was anything but. "I'm not a maniac, Kitty." *But I am when it concerns you.*

Her expression told me she didn't believe me,

that a part of her probably thought I was fucking crazy.

But she didn't press and instead nodded and went back to unpacking the grocery bags. And I just watched her, listened to her tell me what she planned for dinner tonight, how she'd gotten me Tosco's for dessert.

And although I heard every word, the one thought that kept going through my mind was how I planned on finding Josh and hurting him like he fucking hurt *my* woman.

10

Fin

I would've never—had never—done anything that would be considered reckless, that would and could give a bad light to Hawthorne Oil. But the fact that some little prick put his hands on Kitty and hurt her had every single piece of common sense and rational thought leaving me.

And I reveled in it.

If I didn't do this, didn't make that little fucker pay in kind, it would fester inside me until it was a poisonous substance that I'd never get rid of.

I was like that with everything in my life, this need to finish what was started, a positive but also a negative.

I'd left shortly after dinner and had seen on her face that she knew what I was doing, what I planned on doing. And when I got home and if she asked where I'd been, what I'd done, I would tell her the truth. I wasn't going to sugarcoat anything, wasn't going to lie. There was no point.

And I'd already come to the realization that I would handle this tonight, that when I got back to the house, I would sit her down and tell her how I felt. I was done waiting.

She'd only been here a week, yet it felt like a fucking eternity that I'd been holding this in. She could make me wait, could have all the time she needed, but these feelings I had for her needed to be said out loud.

And that needed to be done tonight.

Once in town, I'd driven around to a couple of the spots where I knew the lowlife loitered. I ended up finding the little bastard hanging out in the alleyway between the liquor and convenience stores. He was with one other guy, each of them with a bottle in their hand, cigarettes between their lips. I pulled into a parking spot, my headlights shining directly into the alleyway. For a moment, they didn't pay me any attention, but when I didn't turn the lights off, they both looked in my direction. I had my hands tight around the steering wheel, the leather creaking from the force I was using.

The other guy said something to Josh, tossed his cigarette to the side, and then ended up walking away. But the little motherfucker still watched me after he was alone, this nasty-toothed grin spread across his face.

He flicked his cigarette away and brought his bottle up to his mouth, taking a long drink as he stared at me. He couldn't see me clearly because of the tinted windows, but he'd see me soon enough.

For a second, I sat there and let my rage grow, fester, increase until it consumed me. I'd never felt anything like this, this burning intensity to exact revenge, to let someone know that what they did was wrong... that they'd touched what was mine.

Even if he hadn't put his hands on her, the fact that he approached her, spoke to her, had every possessive instinct in me coming alive. But he had hurt her, marked her, and that I would not stand for.

I climbed out of the car, didn't even bother closing my door or cutting the engine, and made my way toward him.

He was a ballsy fucker, I'd give him that, as he held his ground, his grin growing. I was bigger than him, not just in height but in weight as well. I was double his size and width. He didn't stand a chance. And although I could've easily killed him on principle alone, I was making a point, not just for Kitty, not just to stake my claim, but to put in his mind that him assaulting women would not be tolerated.

I stopped when I was just a foot from him, inhaled deeply, feeling my nostrils flare. He smelled like stale cigarettes and rancid sweat, booze, and despair. He smelled like a fucking piece of shit.

I could've talked to him, could've set him straight with words alone, but that wasn't going to happen, because I knew this man was nothing but a lowlife. He'd do this again and again until someone stopped him.

And that someone was me. That day was today.

"You assaulted what's mine," I growled.

He didn't speak for a moment, but I could see his mind working as he tried to remember or place what I was talking about. Finally, the light went on in his head, and his eyebrows rose slightly for a second.

"You mean that bitch from the grocery store today?"

That was all it took for me to lose my cool, for every sane, rational part of my body to snap in half. I said nothing as I reared my arm back and brought my fist right to the center of his face. I heard bone crunch, his nose breaking.

He dropped the bottle, and I heard the glass break within the paper bag. He cupped his face but not before I saw blood pouring from his nose, smelled it thicken the air with a coppery aroma.

He stumbled back, hunched over slightly, but he still looked at me, a stunned expression on his face. He knew who I was. Everyone in town did.

But he was drunk and high all the time, probably so hopped up on drugs right now that he just didn't care.

I took a step forward and smelled the fear come from him. He finally understood, took notice that I could crush him in my hands as if he were nothing but a nuisance, a fly.

"If you touch, look, even fucking think about what's mine—or another woman again—I'll come looking for you, Josh." I grinned, but it was more of a sneer, a flash of my teeth to let him know I was more animal than man right now.

"There's nowhere you can hide, nowhere you can run that I can't fucking find you. My pockets are endless, black holes of resources, and my reach is far and wide with my connections. I'd find you. And I'll make sure that if you ever do this again, you'll never have function of your arms or legs from that point forward." I stared at him right in the eyes, could see the reality set in, his head clearing from whatever substance he was intoxicated with, so my words really penetrated.

I wasn't a violent man by nature, had never even gotten into a physical fight. I used my words as my weapon. But when you wanted something so fucking much, it consumed you, and you'd do anything to make sure it was safe.

And I felt that way with Kitty.

"Do you understand me?" He nodded quickly, and I heard the grunt of pain come from him as the movement jarred his now broken nose.

I stared him in the eyes for a moment longer, really cementing my words, really making him fucking see how serious I was, before I turned and headed back home.

I felt raw in this moment, my emotions and feelings torn open, as if somebody had cut my chest, exposed my heart.

Yes, tonight I'd let Kitty know she was mine. I'd let her know with my words and with my body that I wasn't letting her go.

11

Kitty

I'd been cleaning up after dinner when I heard Fin come into the kitchen. To say there had been this thickness in the room as we ate would've been an understatement. His expression had been hard, as if he had something heavy on his mind but didn't want to share it with me.

He didn't have to. I knew what the problem was.

I hadn't missed how he kept looking at my wrist. As the hours passed, the bruise started to become more noticeable. He was pissed about it. I knew without him saying those words.

And that had been hours ago. He told me he had to run an errand. I didn't question where he was going so late, because it wasn't my business. But deep in my gut, I knew what was happening, what he was doing.

Going to handle what happened to me... going to find the man who touched me.

I was in my room, pacing, feeling on edge. I didn't want him fighting my battles. I was a strong, independent woman, I kept telling myself. But a part of me, a part that was pretty damn strong, couldn't help the feminine appreciation that he wanted to protect me.

Tonight. When he was back. I'd tell him how I felt.

I couldn't hold it in anymore, not when I knew the looks he gave me, the way he watched me, and now this meant he had to harbor some kind of deeper feelings for me too.

I'd wait for him downstairs. I'd look him in the eyes and be honest, the truth spilling from me without any reservation, without worry or fear. I didn't care if I lost my job over this, because even if I did, at least I'd have the honesty out in the open and the weight off my shoulders.

I descended the stairs, and just as I stepped onto the landing of the main level, the front door opened. Fin stepped in, his gaze focused on the floor as he closed the door behind him. He lifted his head, and our eyes locked.

My heart started beating harder, my body instantly reacting to his presence. But he looked... different. He appeared more primal and on edge than I'd ever seen him before.

I didn't need to ask what was wrong. I knew.

My gaze instantly lowered to his hands, and that's when I saw the knuckles on one of them. Busted and raw... from hitting something or someone.

I lifted my focus back to his face, and a gasp left me when I watched the way he lowered his head, his eyes locked on mine. He started moving toward me, this deep rumble leaving his chest. I found myself taking a step back and gripping the banister of the stairs for support. I may have retreated slightly, but I wasn't running away.

He looked positively animalistic as he stalked forward.

Fin stopped just a few steps from me, and I watched his nostrils flare as he inhaled deeply, as if he were taking in my scent. Another deep sound left him, and I swallowed, feeling on edge, exposed... unsure of what was happening.

It was like electricity moved around us, in us. I

felt the power come from him, the purely male aroma of a man looking at a woman he wanted.

And I was that woman.

"You went after him," I whispered, not even phrasing it as a question, because we both knew the truth. We both knew the answer. He didn't respond, just took another step toward me. But I held my ground, refused to back away even more. I didn't want to. I wanted to be as close to Fin as humanly possible. I'd already told myself tonight was the night to tell him how I felt.

And so I craned my head back to look into his face, stared into his turbulent eyes, and I felt myself falling deeper... felt the attraction become more intense.

No. It was more than just needing him in a primal way. It was more than just sexual desire.

I didn't know what it was. But I knew it controlled me.

I knew it shaped me.

I knew it freed me.

So I just said it, laid it out, bared myself to him heart and soul. And damn the consequences.

"I want you, Fin."

12

Fin

In the next breath, I had her in my arms, no thoughts about consequences or repercussions. I thought I might've hurt her inadvertently, but when she rose up on her toes and pressed her chest more firmly against mine, her belly now digging into my cock, I tilted her head with my hand and knew my girl was into this just as much as I was.

I just wanted to hold her, to finally touch her.

With my hand now tangled in her hair, tilting her head back impossibly farther, I leaned down and slammed my mouth against hers. The surprised sound that left her fueled me on, and I pushed my tongue between the seam of her lips, delving inside, tasting her, feeling her surrender like ink spilling from a jar.

It ignited me, inflamed me.

She wanted me? She had every piece of me.

I kissed her with passion, brutality. I fucked her mouth with my lips and tongue. I made her take every ounce of me, and still, I gave her more.

I moved my hands over her shoulders, along her back, over the feminine, slender dip of her waist and to the flare of her hips. I dug my fingers in for only a second before I moved my palms along to the perfect mounds of her ass. And then I squeezed hard enough that she let out a little sound.

I grunted at the feel of her body against mine, at how feminine she was against my masculinity. My dick was this raging lead pipe barely restrained and confined behind my slacks.

The fucker dug against the material, pressed against my zipper. I knew she felt it, knew that the little mewling noises that came from her as I ground my cock into her belly were from pleasure.

She wanted me inside her. I knew it. Felt it.

She wanted more, was desperate for it. I could smell it coming from her, a sweet arousal that thickened the air, coated me and had me even more fucking turned on.

With my hands still on her ass, my fingers curved around the perfect mounds, I lifted her easily. She moaned and wrapped her legs around my waist, her pussy now in direct contact with my bulge. I mouth-fucked her for long moments, unable to stop myself, unable to tame the passion that I had for her.

"Tell me again that you want me, baby." The words were muffled against her lips.

She moaned and nodded before saying, "I want you so badly."

I wanted to hear her tell me that she needed me over and over again. Because I sure as fuck needed her.

I held her in my arms, her body tiny, her weight slight. I took the stairs two at a time, needing to get her in my room, on my bed. I was desperate for her, hungry... fucking starving.

Once at the top of the steps, I quickly strode to my room, never once breaking the kiss. I was so damn worked up I couldn't even think straight. My lone thought was getting her naked and getting my cock deep in her pussy. I needed to make her come, wanting to know I was the one giving her that pleasure.

I bet her pussy would be so wet that once I finally slid into her tight heat, there'd be absolutely no resistance as I thrust in and out, as I filled every part of her with my thick, big dick.

I knew her little cunt would squeeze my shaft until I felt strangled.

I groaned at how dirty my thoughts had become.

When I was in my room, I didn't even bother shutting the door. There was no point. We were in this house alone, just the two of us, and I was about to fuck the hell out of her.

I strode to the bed with her still in my arms, her hands tangled in my hair as she pulled at the strands forcefully, her desperation clear.

I couldn't even breathe as I continued to kiss her, as I curled my fingers deeper into her hips, slightly pushing her body down on my raging erection. She shifted in my arms as if she were trying to scale my body, her movements making me lose my balance for a second. I turned, landing on the bed, my ass to the mattress, Kitty still in my arms.

"Fuck, Kitty." I was frantic for her, needing her like I needed oxygen, like I needed blood rushing through my veins to give me life.

I slid my hand up her back, cupping her nape,

keeping her pressed to my body, to my lips. She wasn't going anywhere.

Ever.

I'd never been this hard before, never had my balls ache, the need to cum so profound that it stole my very sanity.

I'd never wanted anyone like this, never desired a woman that all I could see was a future with her, having her as my wife, as the mother of my children. It was so strong inside me, that feeling, that need to make it a reality... *my* reality.

Our reality.

She shifted on my lap, our kiss breaking. Her legs spread on either side of my thighs, her chest rising and falling, her breasts brushing along my chest. Motherfucking hell, she felt so good on me. So damn good. The way she looked at me, this little innocent expression on her face, had every possessive feeling in me rising to the nth degree.

Everything inside me went primal. Feral.

I felt crazed, and I didn't stop myself when I reached up and wound my hand in her hair, adding some pressure, bringing her forward again, so close our mouths nearly touched. I took her frantic breaths into my lungs, made her a part of me.

I'd be giving her a part of myself soon enough.

I needed to be gentle, soft, and sweet, because right now, I felt like I could tear Kitty up. My desire for her was a living entity in me, wanting to be brutal, barbaric even.

"Kitty," I groaned her name, loving the way it rolled off my tongue. I felt like I should have been saying it my entire life. "I want to be gentle, but fuck, baby..." I breathed out slowly, grappling with control. "The things I want to do to you, the way I want to make you feel... if I were to tell you, they would have you running away."

She breathed out slowly, as if my words affected her on every level.

Good, she knew how I felt now.

"I'm barely hanging on, baby."

She didn't respond right away, just leaned in until I felt her warm breath brush along my lips. A visible shiver wracked my entire body.

Did she know I could have gotten off with the feel of her on my lap, just come in my fucking slacks as if it were nothing?

"I'm barely hanging on too," she finally said, her lips barely brushing along mine when she spoke. "And you can't scare me away. I want this more than I've ever wanted anything."

I closed my eyes and rested my forehead against hers, trying to grapple for control, to hold off from just letting this go. I didn't want this to end too soon.

Gentle. She deserves all the gentle things.

"I don't need gentle," she whispered, and I wondered if I said those words out loud.

I slid my hand up her back, pulling her in impossibly closer, and tangled my hand in her hair.

I tightened my hold on her hair, an involuntary act, because I was getting strung even tighter, worked up even more. I leaned in and rested my forehead against hers. "All I can feel, smell, taste, is you, baby." I wanted to drown in her scent.

I ran my tongue along her lips. I groaned at her taste. I'd never tasted anything sweeter.

"I'm so wet, Fin."

Christ. She was going to have me exploding before I was even inside her tight body.

I hummed harshly, and she started to rock back and forth on me, her hands on my shoulders, her breathing coming in short pants.

Fuck.

"That feel good, baby?"

She closed her eyes and nodded, her head tipping back slightly, her long hair swaying from her movements. She kept rocking on me, and I felt beads of sweat dot my forehead as I strained to gather my control, to not come.

When that happened, I'd be buried deep in her body.

"That's it," I found myself saying and had my hands on her waist, guiding her movements, having her rock back and forth faster. I pushed her lower body down on me at the same time I slightly rose up, grinding my shaft against her.

"Ah," she whispered.

"Give it to me." I hadn't meant to say that out loud, but she started really working herself on me then.

I let go of her waist and placed my palms flat on the bed, leaning my upper body back slightly and letting her do her thing.

We might've had our clothes on still, but I swore to fuck I felt her pussy against my dick as if we were totally naked.

Knowing she was about to get off because of me had pre-cum spilling from the tip of my cock and dampening the front of my slacks.

I wanted to fuck her badly.

"Come for me, Kitty. Let me see you get off."

And she gave into me so damn easily.

She parted her lips, dug her nails into my shoulders painfully—fucking perfectly—and gave me what I wanted.

She came on my demand.

I watched her come, and I swore to fucking everything that was holy that it was almost as good as finding my own release. It felt so fucking good knowing I made her feel this pleasure.

It was long moments as she rode out that wave of ecstasy before she finally settled and relaxed. I wasn't nearly done with her. Not even fucking close.

I cupped the back of her head and tipped it upward so she was looking at me. She finally opened her eyes, this post-euphoric expression on her drowsy face. God, she was gorgeous.

All. Fucking. Mine.

I slammed my mouth on hers, kissing Kitty until she moaned for me and opened her mouth wider. She kissed me back more forcefully, as if she needed to crawl inside me, as if she couldn't get enough.

I stroked my tongue along hers, plunged it into her mouth, and made a guttural sound when she sucked on it. *Christ.*

She pulled away, and I made a deep noise of dissatisfaction. I didn't want to stop, not ever.

I lowered my gaze to her mouth, loving that her lips were red and swollen, a light glossy sheen covering them. I lifted my hand and ran my finger over her bottom lip, pulling the flesh slightly down and letting it go so it slipped back into place.

"Perfect," I murmured. My cock jerked when I pushed my thumb between her lips. "Suck on it," I demanded, my voice low. She sucked on the pad instantly, obeying me, having me growl in approval.

"Are you mine, Kitty?" God, I fucking needed her to say she was.

She ran her tongue over my thumb one last time before letting it slip from her lips. She stared into my eyes, her lips parted, her chest rising and falling. "Yes," she breathed out. "I'm your—"

"Only mine," I finished for her, and she licked her lips and nodded.

"Only yours, Fin."

That's fucking right.

I pulled her in close, claiming her mouth in a searing kiss. I felt the flames singe me from the inside out. I was surprised—proud of my fucking self, if I were being honest—that I'd lasted this long without getting off.

I curled my bigger body around hers, the feel of her perfect handful-sized breasts right against my chest, her nipples hard, had my cock jerking like the fucker had a mind of its own.

I kept my hands on her waist, keeping her right where she was but pressing her down on my dick even harder.

I was going to destroy her in the best of ways.

13

Kitty

F in watched me, stared at me with such intensity I felt it to my core. There was only one word to describe the way Fin looked at me —possessively.

And I loved it. I never wanted him to look at me any other way.

"Only yours, Fin."

I'd actually said those words to him, but what was even more insane was the fact that I *meant* them.

The way I rocked myself against him, moving over his thickness, his massive cock, had me so hungry for him I wanted Fin to consume every part of my being. My pussy was wet, my panties soaked.

My nipples were so hard the tips ached. I wanted him to suck on them, to make my nipples harder, to draw the blood to the surface.

I wanted all of that and more, yet I had no experience in any of this.

I was a virgin.

I wasn't ashamed of my lack of sexual experience. I prided myself that I waited for the right guy, for the right time.

And that time was now.

The right man was Fin.

He made this low sound deep within his chest and tumbled out my name as if it were a lifeline. His dick pressed between my thighs, a huge, thick rod that had my pussy clenching. I was seconds away from begging him to be with me already.

"I've never done this before," I blurted out unceremoniously and felt his entire body stiffen. I waited for his response, maybe his shock, maybe him telling me we should slow down or, God forbid, stop.

"My sweet, innocent little virgin," he groaned and slanted his mouth back down on mine.

I was surprised at how pleased he sounded with my admission, as if he'd been wanting to hear that his entire life.

My body tingled, fire racing along my skin. He

lifted his hips up, digging his dick farther against me, and I gasped.

"I should be gentle with you, such an innocent little thing, Kitty."

I was so ready for him.

He leaned in, and when I felt his tongue along the arch of my neck, I closed my eyes and let my head fall back. He licked and sucked, gently suckling at my flesh. *God, yes.*

Fin was all hard, big, and strong, with bulging muscles. I was so tiny as I sat on his lap, straddled his waist, and felt how hard he was for me.

God, his cock felt *big.*

"I could just do this all night and get off, Kitty. Just holding you, licking you, smelling your sweet flesh." He emphasized his point by inhaling deeply.

I was dizzy, lightheaded from my desire for him. I couldn't handle much more, yet I didn't want this to stop.

"I want to touch you," I found myself saying before I could stop myself. I hadn't meant to say those words out loud, but there they were, hanging between us.

"I'm yours to do with as you please. Touch all of me, baby."

His focus was on my lips, and I licked them involuntarily, or maybe I did it on purpose. Maybe I wanted his focus on that erogenous zone.

I glanced down and saw how big his bulge was. I felt a little intimidated, and maybe he read my mind or saw my expression, because he moved his hands between us and undid the button then pulled the zipper down, freeing his erection. He gripped the base, and my mouth dried, my throat tightened, and I snapped my focus up to his face.

"Okay, baby. Touch me."

The breath I hadn't realized I'd been holding in left me on a *whoosh*, and I obeyed him instantly.

I reached between us with a shaking hand and wrapped my fingers around his shaft. This rough groan left him at that first touch. He was hot and oh so hard, so thick I couldn't even touch my fingers together as I held him. And he was hot. God, he was so hot in my palm.

I was transfixed by the sight of him, how his balls were huge and a heavy weight under the thick, long length. I started stroking him gently, watching as I pleasured him.

"*Goddamn,*" he said hoarsely.

I didn't slow, didn't stop looking at what I did to

him. I moved my hand faster, my mouth parting as I added more pressure. I watched as a dot of clear fluid lined the top of his shaft, and something moved through me to be more wanton. I slid my palm over the flared head and heard him hiss. I used his pre-cum as lubrication as I jerked him off.

I was so wet, so turned on watching him get this pleasure, knowing I was the cause of it. And as I started moving my hand faster up and down his length, as I heard his groans become harsher, more frantic in nature, I knew he was going to come. I knew I was going to get him off.

And so I renewed my efforts, wanting to see him explode, wanting that whiteness to cover my hand. I wanted the knowledge that I'd been the one to break Finland Hawthorne's control.

"You already have, sweetheart," he growled, and I snapped my gaze up to his face.

Had I said those words out loud? God, mortification filled me.

He gently pushed my hand away and shook his head. "If you keep that up, I'll come, and although I know I'll be able to get rock-hard again, the first time I get off with you is going to be when I'm buried deep in your pussy."

He stared at me for a long moment before he said, "How ready are you for me?"

"I'm ready," I said truthfully.

I'm so ready to be fucked by Fin.

14

Fin

I was off the bed and had her back to the mattress seconds later. All I'd needed to hear was how much she wanted me, those words spilling from her mouth like an auditory orgasm.

I forced myself to retreat a step back so I could control myself, so I didn't mount her like some feral creature. Because I sure as fuck wanted to. And the sight of her on my bed, her body seeming dwarfed in my massive mattress, the fact that my scent surrounded her, that she'd now forever stay in this bed, because I wouldn't have it any other way, turned me on even more.

She still wore her clothes, which really wouldn't

fucking do. I needed her naked, needed to bask in her nudity, memorize every inch of her, every dip and hollow. I wanted to know where every birthmark was, how pink her nipples got when she came, if they darkened up even more.

God, I wanted to know all of it.

All her secrets. All her whispered words when she was in the throes of pleasure.

And I'd find out it all, because I wasn't letting her go.

She knew what I wanted without me having to ask. I could see that realization on her face. Or maybe the fact that she kept lowering her eyes to my cock, which was still hard as granite and sticking through the fly of my slacks, was indication enough I wanted to fuck her good and hard.

I needed to feel her tight virgin pussy squeezing my cock. I wanted her to say she was mine while my big, thick dick was buried deep inside her. I wanted to look in her eyes and tell her with my body she was the only one I want.

And as I watched her get undressed, when I saw she was about to toss her little white panties to the floor, I snagged them and brought them to my nose. I inhaled her sweet scent before shoving the underwear in my back pocket.

"Spread your legs, Kitty." I started getting undressed too and never took my eyes off her. When my shirt was off and my pants nothing more than a pile of material on the floor, I reached for my dick and started stroking the fucker again.

And she watched me the whole time.

I lowered my gaze to the perfect mounds of her tits, along her belly, her navel, and right down to her spread pussy. She shaved, not all of it, but enough that her lips were bare and the only hair was a strip at the top of her mound.

Fuck.

She was pink and so damn smooth, and her wetness glistened for me. I sure as fuck wanted to be gentle and go slow. This was her first time, and she deserved candles and silk, soft music and coaxing touches.

She deserved everything I'd never been.

But I'd try. I wanted to be softer around the edges for Kitty.

I wanted to be a gentler man for *her*.

I got on the bed and moved between her thighs, running my hands over her calves, up the back of her thighs, and felt her skin pucker from my touch. "So receptive," I murmured. I settled myself over her much smaller body, my lips at her throat as I started to lick and suck at her flesh. She smelled good, tasted even better.

I should have won a fucking medal for the amount of restraint I was using right now, for the fact that I wasn't thrusting into her welcoming virgin heat. But I could go slow, as slow as humanly possible for a man who was obsessed with a woman.

I was on top of her a second later, had my mouth on her neck, and used my lower half to nudge her thighs open even more so I could wedge myself between them. A guttural sound left me, rising up deep from my body. I knew she felt the vibrations, a physical reminder of what she did to me.

I pressed my cock between her legs, because I couldn't fucking help myself, and felt her slick folds surround my shaft. *Holy shit.* Soaked. She was drenched for me.

I hissed as I started moving back and forth, working myself between her legs, her folds framing my dick, her moans and my grunts fueling me on.

I couldn't stop myself from groaning out my pleasure. "So good," I whispered. "So fucking good, Kitty." I opened my eyes to see hers were closed, as if she couldn't help herself either. I wanted her lost in me.

When I started moving faster, she writhed

beneath me, her mouth parted, her eyes still closed as she was clearly enjoying this moment.

As much as I wanted to keep this going, just let my cock push into her tight body, I wanted to taste her more right now. I needed her flavor on my tongue, sliding down the back of my throat.

I just needed her.

When I slowed, she opened her eyes, this hazy look on her face. I moved down the length of her body, watching her the entire time, going slow so she knew my intent. When my face was right between her thighs, her musky, intoxicating scent slamming into my nose and filling my head, I closed my eyes and inhaled even deeper. I lifted my gaze and stared at her, and saw she watched me expectantly. "Anyone ever touch you like this, baby?"

She didn't verbally respond, just shook her head slowly.

Good, I'll be her first... everything.

I kept my gaze locked on hers as I dragged my tongue through her cleft, starting from her pussy hole to her clit. Over and over, I did this, licking her, lapping her up like she was an ice cream melting on one hot fucking day.

She tasted a hell of a lot better though. Addicting. Intoxicating.

I placed a hand on her belly when she started moving her lower half, squirming slightly as if she couldn't help herself. I fucking loved that she worked herself on my mouth. Her flavor exploded along my tongue, and I hummed in approval.

"Fin!" she cried out my name when I sucked her clit into my mouth.

I licked and sucked on her, knowing I'd never get enough. I wanted to have my face buried between her thighs forever.

There was no stopping me, nothing able to sate me in this moment. I needed all of Kitty. And to ease some of the pressure in my cock and balls, I started dry humping the bed, moving my hips against the mattress, thrusting myself on the sheets like a fucking teenager trying to get off.

"Oh," she said softly as if in surprise, and she really started working herself against my mouth at the same time she buried her hands in my hair. I groaned at how good it felt to feel her touching me while I ate her out. I knew she was going to come for me, and so I renewed my efforts.

I rolled my hips, moving my cock almost violently against the bed, because I was so fucking worked up.

"Fin... God, Fin I'm coming." Those words were a

broken cry from her as she pulled at my hair and gave it all to me.

I sucked her clit hard and rode out the orgasm with her, never stopping until she gasped and gently pushed at my head. I gave her pussy one more long lick before pulling away, rising up, and grabbing my dick. I stroked that thick, huge fucker from root to tip, used my pre-cum to lube myself up, and had my focus trained right on her exposed pussy.

I tasted her.

I smelled her.

She surrounded me.

"I want more," she said and reached out for me. I rested my chest to hers, laced the tip of my cock right at her pussy, and stared into her eyes. I took her mouth in another hard, deep kiss, making her taste herself on my tongue. She dug her nails into the skin of my waist, pulling me closer, kissing me just as desperately as I was kissing her.

I leaned back, bracing my hands beside her, looking down at her. She was so fucking gorgeous, her pussy pink and wet, swollen from me eating her out.

The tip of my cock was still nudging her opening, and as I stared down at her, I started to push in. I stilled when only the head was partially lodged in and stared into her eyes. "Tell me you're mine. Only mine."

She licked her lips, her fingers flexing against me slightly. "I don't want to ever be anyone else's."

"That's fucking right. You won't ever be anyone else's, not if I have anything to do with it."

And then in one fluid move, I buried my dick in her wet, tight virgin pussy.

Mine.

That lone word reverberated in my head over and over again, seeping into me until it was now a part of my being.

I'd felt that resistance of her innocence, power washing through me that no one would ever be able to claim her virginity but me.

It was mine.

She was mine.

Kitty gasped, her pain clear, and my heart broke at knowing I was the cause of her discomfort. I vowed from this point on to only make her feel good.

I cupped the side of her face and stilled, letting her get accustomed to my size, to being inside her. I was a big man overall, and I knew being buried in her—especially her being a virgin—was a shock to her body.

"Are you okay?" I tried to say those words in the gentlest tone possible.

She nodded just as her pussy clenched around my cock. I groaned at the brutal pleasure she brought out in me. "I'm okay." She lifted her arms and wrapped them around my shoulders, and I leaned in to kiss her softly. I'd give her all the time in the world.

"You want to stop?"

"God, no."

Thank fuck, because pulling out of her would have been the hardest thing I'd ever done in my life.

I gave her one more lingering kiss before I started moving. I swore she became even wetter with each thrust I gave her. I rose up on my forearms, so my upper body was now off hers, and looked down at where I was buried. I pulled my cock out so just the tip was lodged in her pussy and saw how wet my length was, could even see the streaks of her innocence on me.

God, that made me feel... so many fucking things.

I nearly came right then.

I kept that slow pace for so long I felt my heart race so hard I wouldn't have been surprised if the damn organ busted through my chest.

I pushed in deep and nearly fucking lost it.

"Oh," she gasped, and her eyes widened. I stilled, but she dug her nails into my skin. "Don't stop. It feels good."

The display of pleasure moving across her face was unmistakable, but I wanted to see more. I wanted to see her delirious from it.

And so I pushed into her once more before stilling. I felt her inner muscles ripple around me before she finally relaxed. I knew it had to hurt her, and that fucking tore at me. I didn't want to cause her any pain, but I couldn't help the proprietary claim that washed over me.

No other man would experience her like this.

"I want more," she whispered as she stared into my eyes.

I'd give her everything.

And so I started rocking back and forth, pushing my cock into her slowly and pulling it out. I kept a steady, even pace, knowing she needed to get used to me. But as the seconds moved by, my control was slipping. I felt more beads of sweat line my temple, cover my back. It wasn't just because I was fucking Kitty, but because I was losing all my control.

"Fuck, I'm going to come." I hadn't meant to say

that out loud. I felt like it made me weak, unable to hold off until my woman could find her release.

But fuck, she feels too good.

"Me too," she moaned and closed her eyes, her lips parting as she groaned.

Hearing those words come from her gave my body a mind of its own. I picked up my speed, swinging my hips back and forth, tunneling my cock in and out of her pussy. I was mindless in my need to get us both off. I gritted my teeth, but before I allowed myself that pleasure, Kitty would have hers first.

I reached between our bodies, found her engorged little clit, and started rubbing it. She gasped, and I knew how sensitive she must've been.

"Come on, darling. Come for me." And then I felt her tense, felt her pussy milk my cock in hard pulses. She tossed her head back, her neck straining, a low cry leaving her. The fact that she was coming *for me* —because of me—would have me following after her.

"You feel so damn good." Fuck, I couldn't even think, let alone get those words out coherently.

I was going to come, even though I wanted this feeling with Kitty to last for the rest of my fucking life. There was no way I could hold off a second longer. I'd already tested my control the moment she stepped through the threshold of my house.

The pleasure consumed me, took over until I was its slave, until I had no choice but to submit. I'd never allowed anything or anyone to have power over me, but Kitty was the one person who could bend me like no other.

I slammed my dick into her welcoming, tight heat, and her body slid up the bed an inch. She reached back and gripped the slats of the head- board, her neck arched, her chest thrust out.

"You're going to take every ounce of me," I growled as I shoved into her one last time, feeling her pussy still quiver around my dick, and I finally let go.

I tipped my head back and roared out my release. I sounded like a fucking wounded animal as it came from me. I forced my eyes open so I could look at Kitty, watch as she took all of me. And she did... every last damn inch.

The high took me to the fucking stars. Never in my life had I felt this good, not in pleasure, not in anything I'd ever done. And I knew why.

Because Kitty was the missing piece to my life, the one thing I'd always needed but didn't know I'd been without until I saw her. She didn't even have to be physically in front of me to know she was mine. That one picture had been all it took.

As my pleasure dimmed and waned, I finally allowed myself to breathe. I let myself fall to the mattress unceremoniously, the air sawing in and out of my lungs. I could have fallen asleep right then and there, content and sated for the first time in my life.

I turned my head and looked at her, seeing she already watched me with this pleasure-hazed expression on her face. Her cheeks were pink, her lips red and swollen from my kisses, and her eyes glossy from her post-orgasmic high.

God... I loved this woman. I truly fucking did.

I was part of her now... and Kitty was a part of me.

She wielded all the control over me. All of it.

I didn't know if Kitty truly understood that she was mine, but I'd sure as hell remind her every day of my fucking life.

"You're the first woman I've been with in years, Kitty, *years*." Hell, I would wager it had been at least a decade, but I wouldn't go into it further. I'd told her, because I wanted her to know. I wanted her to know I'd waited, because I knew there was something more, something perfect out there. I just hadn't known it until she came into my life.

She smiled and leaned in to kiss me. I'd taken her virginity, her innocence. It was forever mine.

She was forever mine.

I pulled her close, needing her like this always. A contented, pleasurable sigh left her, and she rested her head on my chest. It was perfection having her here with me, against my body, filled with my cum... marked by me.

My cock hardened again, and I heard her gasp as it started to dig into her belly.

"Again?" she whispered in this drowsy yet very clearly ready-for-me voice.

"Always," I growled. "We're just getting started for the night, baby."

And the grin she gave me told me she was on the same page.

15

Kitty

The next morning

I slowly opened my eyes, the sun coming through the partially pulled curtains and washing over me, an invisible blanket of heat and comfort. I knew I was alone in the bed before I turned my head and looked to where Fin had been sleeping. This longing took place right in the center of my chest, this pressure, this emptiness.

I rolled onto my back, the scent of Fin enveloping me. God, he smelled good, and I felt him still, all over me... in me. Between my thighs was sore, sensitive in all the intimate places that reminded me of what we'd done last night. The fact that he was the one who now owned my virginity, that I was the one who ended his celibacy, had a surge of desire washing through me again.

I might be sore, but I could have him all over again and still ask for more.

I don't know how long I lay there, but I knew it was still pretty early in the morning. I was about to get up when the bedroom door opened. I brought the blanket to my chest, not quite sure why I was shielding myself, since it was only the two of us at the house. And Fin walked in holding a tray, the smell of bacon and coffee instantly filling my nose.

The smile he gave me actually had my heart skipping a beat. I couldn't even describe it accurately, but he looked like a man who was so damn happy to see me, like I just made his world.

I sat up, the sheets still covering my chest as he came fully into the room. He walked around the bed so he was sitting on the edge right beside me, his focus on me. He looked like he couldn't take his eyes off me, and I felt my face heat from how much he watched me.

I moved over slightly so he could place the tray next to me. Looking down at the spread, I felt warm at his thoughtfulness. He made everything. There were pancakes and scrambled eggs, bacon and fresh fruit. There were even a couple slices of buttered toast, and a large glass of what I knew was fresh-squeezed orange juice beside the plate.

"Fin, you made this all for me?"

"Of course," he said, and his smile brightened. He looked different. I couldn't quite place it or figure out what the difference was, but then it hit me.

He looked truly happy.

It was as if he found something that he'd lost.

It was such a strange moment, knowing what we'd done last night, what we'd said to each other, and now this morning. In just a small amount of time that had passed since I started working for him, he'd changed. I remembered how he'd been that first day, so growly and hardened, as if he had this massive chip on his shoulder.

He would always be rough around the edges, this immovable Viking, this giant. But right now, this man in front of me... it was like I was seeing a different side of him.

And I felt like he was the man I'd been looking for my entire life.

My cheeks heated all over again at that thought. This seemed so... permanent, as if what we shared last night was more than what I could ever imagine. Sure, he'd spoken to me so intimately, shared bits about himself, the words he said so possessively. But I wondered if that had all been said in the heat of the moment.

I hadn't realized I was staring down at my lap until I felt his finger under my chin, until I felt him lift my head up so I was looking into his eyes again. Gone was that joyous expression and in its place was one of a serious nature.

I swallowed roughly at the intensity I suddenly felt from him. "What does this all mean?" My voice was soft, like a feather blowing in the wind. Did he even hear me? Had I even said it out loud? He closed his eyes.

He exhaled and opened his eyes a second later, his gaze so turbulent, so full of concentration. I could practically see his mind turning over, wondering what he was about to say right now. All kinds of fear slammed into me, things like he'd say this had all been a one-time thing. Words about how I'd lost my job because we crossed boundaries.

Sure, those things terrified me, but the thing that gripped me the tightest, stole my breath, and squeezed my heart was the fear that he would tell me he didn't want me, that what he felt for me wasn't even a fraction of what I felt for him.

Because the truth was... I had fallen for him. I'd

fallen in love with him. It was insane and ludicrous, almost unbelievable. But I'd never felt anything realer in my life.

"It means I'm not letting you go, Kitty."

His words were like this bucket of frigid water over me, causing my spine to straighten, having goose bumps form along my skin. It wasn't a bad feeling. They were words that woke me up, ones that jumpstarted my heart.

"It means you're mine, that everything I said last night was the truth. It means so much more than anything I could ever speak in the English language."

I didn't know what to say, didn't know how to accurately describe my feelings.

Telling him I'd fallen in love with him seemed almost rushed, as if he'd think I was crazy for having such strong emotions for someone so quickly. But the way he looked at me, the way he spoke, it all seemed like he felt the same way.

"It means that I want you in my life." He leaned in slowly, so he was now more eye-level with me. "Do you understand what I'm saying? Do you understand how deeply I mean these words?"

I licked my lips and nodded slowly. What was I agreeing to?

"Tell me what that means to you, Kitty."

I blew out a slow breath of air, knowing I couldn't lie, couldn't hide how I felt. It would just eat away at me. Besides, after what we shared and experienced last night, after hearing what Fin just told me, I wanted to be just as honest with him.

"It means forever."

The sound that came from him was purely male. "It fucking means forever, baby." And then he broke into a huge grin, his straight, white teeth flashing right before he leaned in and kissed me, stole the air from me, made me delirious from my passion and my love.

He broke away only long enough to pull me onto his lap, the food now forgotten, the blanket and sheet sliding completely from my body, so I now straddled him naked. But I didn't care. I'd never felt so light and free in my life. I never felt like I belonged anywhere as much as I did with Fin.

And it looked like we were really doing this. It looked like I was giving myself to this man, and he was giving himself to me.

And I'd never looked more forward to the future than I did right now.

EPILOGUE ONE
FIN

Fin

Several months later

Manual labor. That was what I resorted to in order to make my woman happy. But hell, if my girl wanted a garden in the backyard, a trellis for grapes, even though I told her they probably wouldn't grow well, given our location, the lack of sun, and a handful of other obstacles, my woman got whatever she wanted.

So here I was, bringing my hammer down over and over again, building the raised beds so she could plant tomatoes and cucumbers, green beans and squash. I was pretty sure she wanted to plant more than just grapes, so I'd build her twenty if that was what it took to see her smile.

It was only when the sun started to set that I put my tools away and looked at my progress. I felt proud, not because I built this shit by hand, but because I knew it would make her happy.

That was my purpose in life... making her happy.

I turned and was about to head back toward the house when the image of Kitty in the sunroom had me stopping. My breath caught at the way she looked with the setting sun coming through the break in the trees, how the light created this halo and glow around her.

Everything I felt for her was genuine. Authentic. My love for her was fierce. It could never be tamed. And the love I had for her was endless.

I watched as she rose on her toes to water one of the hanging baskets, a spider plant she bought a couple months ago in town. Her shirt rose up slightly, and I saw the swatch of creamy skin exposed and looked at that little indentation of her belly button.

I was rock-hard in a matter of seconds.

There was a deep noise that surrounded me, reminiscent of thunder. I realized it came from me, this almost war song of my need for Kitty.

I had one purpose, one intent—get to my woman and make her feel good.

I was in the sunroom before she even knew it, stood behind her, and had my hands gripping her waist. She gasped and looked over her shoulder, and I knew, just the look on my face, she knew what I wanted. After taking the watering can from her and setting it aside, I undid my button and pulled the zipper down on my jeans.

"You're all dirty and sweaty," she breathed out, but I could tell she wasn't worried about that.

"And I bet your cunt is wet for me because of those facts, isn't it?" It wasn't really a question, because I knew the answer.

She moaned her response.

I didn't even bother pushing my jeans down, just pulled my hard cock out through the fly and stroked myself from root to tip as I waited for her to shimmy out of her shorts and panties. This wasn't going to be a romantic coupling.

It was going to be fast and hard. I was going to fuck Kitty until she couldn't walk comfortably tomorrow.

She looked over her shoulder again, and I gripped her chin with my forefinger and thumb, keeping her in place as I slammed my mouth down on hers.

I kissed her for long seconds, running my tongue along her lips, plunging it into her mouth. When I broke away, it was to press my hand on the center of her back and shove her upper body forward as I pulled her lower half out more. I kicked her legs out and leaned back to look at her exposed pussy.

"Yeah, that's the sweet fucking spot," I groaned. "All mine." I ran my fingers through her wet slit and heard her moan softly. I knew there was no way I was going to last once I was in there. "You want my big cock in your tight little pussy, Kitty baby?"

"Just fuck me, Fin. I'm soaking wet."

Fuck.

I gripped her ass and spread it wide, taking a long look at the pink, soaking center of her cunt and the right little hole of her ass. My cock jerked again, and my balls drew up tight. I needed this like I needed to breathe. There was fog on the glass in front of her from her frantic breathing, and I knew she wouldn't last once I was inside her either.

Taking my cock in hand, I led the head to her pussy hole. Instantly, her heat enveloped me, and I clenched my jaw. My balls drew up, the sack heavy. I was going to fill her up with as much cum as I had for her.

I grabbed her hair, yanked her head back, baring her throat, and plunged my cock into her in one hard, thorough thrust. Kitty arched her back and opened her mouth on a silent cry. I felt her cunt stretch around me, and my balls drew up even more, slapping against her pussy.

Damn. She felt good.

I slid all the way in, getting my cock nice and juicy from her lust, then pulled out, allowing just the tip to stay at the entrance. I gave myself a second to gather control before I shoved back in hard. Her upper body pushed hard against the glass, her hands flat on either side of her so she could steady herself for my fucking.

Her pussy was so tight, so wet and hot.

I started pounding into her and retreating. The sound of my flesh slapping hers filled the sunroom, surrounding us.

"You always feel so fucking good, baby." I grinned and closed my eyes. "I'm not going to last." I grabbed her hips harder, digging my fingers into her flesh, knowing she'd wear my bruises.

I was making hard, deep noises. She made soft, mewling ones.

I reached around and found her clit with my finger, teasing that little bundle, knowing she'd get off for me if I kept this up.

"I need you to get off, darling. I'm so damn close to filling you up." I plunged my cock in and out of her at the same time I rubbed her clit back and forth. I needed to feel her pussy clamping down on my shaft, milking me as if she were thirsty for my seed.

"I'm coming," she cried out and rested her cheek on the glass, her eyes closed, and her lips parted as she rode out her pleasure.

She cried my name softly right before she finally went over the edge. I'd felt the first tremors of her orgasm ripple around my cock, and I started pumping into her faster, slamming my shaft deep into her and making her cry out over and over again.

And then I couldn't hold off the inevitable anymore.

I came so fucking hard I saw lights in front of me. I rode that fucking pleasure like my life depended on it. I filled her up with my cum like she needed to be marked by me from the inside out.

And only when I felt the ecstasy start to let me have my sanity back did I pull out of her.

We both sighed in contentment, and I brought

my lips to the back of her head, kissing her softly. I felt her tremble for me. The sweat started to cool and dry on my body. Even though I was spent, my cock started to harden again as I remembered the pleasure only Kitty could give me.

Immediately, I had my hand between her thighs, my palm cupping her pussy so my seed stayed right where it was supposed to.

Inside my woman.

I growled low when she shivered from my touch. She turned so she was now facing me, and I placed my hand right back between her thighs, my cum starting to slowly slip from her tight pussy. I slid my fingers up and down her slit, coating her with my seed, marking her even more. She smelled like me in every conceivable way.

"I love you," I murmured, inhaling the sweet scent of Kitty. "Tell me you love me." I pushed a thick finger into her, and she parted her lips and hummed softly. I wanted to hear her say it over and over again. I knew I sure as hell told her so much she probably got sick of hearing the words spill from my mouth.

"I love you so much, Fin." She licked her lips, and I saw the pleasure start to peak in her again. "And you're stuck with me."

I grinned as I started finger-fucking her. "Baby, you were mine before you even knew it. I knew you were mine the moment I saw your photo and application. So, Kitty, *you're* the one stuck with *me*."

She chuckled and shook her head but then closed her eyes and moaned as I thrust my fingers in and out of her faster.

"You always have to have the last word on this, don't you?"

I hummed low and leaned in, kissing her as I made her come again.

When it concerned her, I sure as hell did. Because she'd never love me as much as I loved her.

And then I gripped her ass and lifted her off the ground. She wrapped her thighs around my waist, and just like that, I slid my cock back into her.

Mine.

EPILOGUE TWO

Fin
One year later

The soft sound of her laughter always had my gut clenching and my heart racing. Even all this time later, just one look at Kitty could light up my entire world.

I'd never believed in soulmates, didn't really think destiny or fate was something a man needed to succeed in life. I'd always thought working hard, being diligent, independent, and going after what you wanted was how you got to the finish line and everything you wanted.

How wrong I'd been.

Because one look at Kitty when I'd first seen her

picture, and I'd known all of that had been false. I'd been so wrong.

I looked over at her, her body spread out along the leather couch, her feet on my lap as I gently massaged them. The blanket she had over her legs had slipped down her belly, exposing the slight roundness of her stomach.

I felt a smile form along my lips at the sight of her shirt having ridden up slightly. The fact that she was starting to show had male pride and satisfaction filling me. It was like this primal, animalistic sensation knowing *I* was the one who put a baby in her, knowing *I* was the one who had her belly growing big like that.

I didn't stop myself from reaching out and placing a hand on her stomach. She didn't look at me, just laughed at something on the TV and placed her hand over mine. After long moments, she finally turned her eyes in my direction, her fingers trailing over my much larger ones.

"I love you," I said, probably for the twentieth time today alone. I told her every chance I got, every passing, during every meal. I couldn't say it enough.

"I love you too."

Those three words didn't even accurately describe what I felt for her, how strongly I'd fight for her. And so maybe that's why I told her all the time. Maybe that's why I wanted to cement those words between us over and over until there was no doubt of my declaration to her.

I rested my head back on the couch and stared at the TV. The movie that was playing with something she picked out, a "rom-com" she called it. All I knew was I couldn't focus on anything but her.

The feel of her body next to mine.

The heat coming from her.

My love for her.

I continued to rub her feet with my free hand, running my fingers along the arch, over her little toes. Her nails were painted this peach color, almost the same shade as her skin. If I could marry this girl again, I would in a heartbeat. But we'd had one hell of a wedding, a massive gathering that had brought everyone I knew, everyone I was connected with to the celebration.

Her side had been small and intimate, and although I wondered if that bothered her, she never told me otherwise, never looked anything less than happy to be surrounded by people who were genuinely happy for us.

I spared no expense for the wedding, wanting

the very best despite her saying she didn't need anything fancy or big.

I'd scoffed.

I'd give her the moon—the world—if that's what she wanted. And now a year later, we were starting a family.

Our family.

Before she'd gotten pregnant, I'd taken a step back from the business, because I wanted to spend more time with her. Now that we were going to have a baby, I'd taken an even further step back. Although I still handled all the important aspects of Hawthorne Oil, these were the truly important moments in my life.

Spending time with her. Watching as she grew big with our little one. And of course telling her I loved her a hundred times a day.

I'd never sell the company, and in fact hoped that one day I could pass it down to our children to run. But being as hands-on as I had been wasn't an option anymore. It wasn't even a desire for me.

"I love you so much," she said.

I looked over at her just as she lifted the corner of her mouth in a sweet smile. "Not as much as I love you."

She lifted an eyebrow in challenge and rose up,

leaning toward me so she could place her lips on mine.

"That might be up for debate," she whispered against my lips, and I chuckled softly before gently wrapping my hands around her hips and hauling her onto my lap.

She had her legs on either side of my waist, and I felt no shame that I was already hard for her, my cock digging into the soft valley between her thighs. She started seductively rocking against me, her pupils dilating, her mouth parting as a soft moan left her.

I knew my woman was just as insatiable as I was. And like I did every single time I held her, as I looked into her eyes, I fell in love with Kitty all over again.

Kitty

Ten years later

A decade. That's what we were celebrating. Ten glorious, wonderful years of marriage with the man I loved more each day. He was not only our provider and our protector, but also the stealer of my heart, the lover of my body, and the father of my children.

In a decade, our life had grown exponentially. We had three children—two boys who were spitting images of their father, and a little girl, who had my eyes but her father's stubbornness.

Hawk, our oldest, was already so invested in the family business that I knew one day he'd run Hawthorne Oil.

Theo, our middle son, was so smart he could solve problems grown men couldn't even wrap their heads around.

And then there was Ivy, our baby girl who played the piano and had an affinity for wildlife and all the creatures that inhabited the world. She was our gentle soul, our animal whisperer. And boy did she have the men in her life wrapped around her little finger. All she had to do was look at them with those big, blue, puppy dog eyes and they were putty in her hands.

Our house was full and happy, the sound of our babies' laughter something I woke up to every morning and fell asleep to every night. Of course there were ups and downs, arguments and disagreements, but it made us all stronger.

Because the man who currently held me was what I was truly thankful for. Without him, I'd have none of this.

I closed my eyes and let the soft sway of the boat rock me into contentment.

Fin had planned an extravagant ten-year anniversary trip for us. My parents were watching the kids, and he'd swept me away to the Mediterranean. For two weeks, we'd been sailing from coast to coast, visiting little villages and towns, eating exotic foods, and sunbathing on the beaches as we listened to the waves lapping at the shore.

Never in my wildest dreams would I have ever thought this would be my life. But it wasn't about money or notoriety. It wasn't about status or power. It was about having this man by my side, creating our family, and watching our children grow.

It was about making memories.

I opened my eyes and lifted my arm, seeing the bracelet wrapped loosely around my wrist. He'd bought it for me yesterday at this little fishing village. It hadn't been anything expensive and wasn't elaborate. But it was handmade, with little glass detailed beads around silk rope. And Fin had gotten it for me, because he said the blue beads reminded him of my eyes.

I smiled at that memory and felt his hold around me tighten, as if he'd heard my thoughts.

"I love you," he said in a husky, grumbly voice.

I shifted on the bed so I could look into his face, cupped his scruff-covered jaw, and leaned in to kiss him. "Not as much as I love you."

He snorted, but I felt him smile against my mouth.

"That's up for debate."

Now I was the one who laughed softly.

Yeah, I guess it was, but we had the rest of our lives to "fight" on it, and what an incredible thing to have to worry about.

The End

Enjoy an excerpt from **The Vessel**, a new contemporary romance from Jenika Snow!

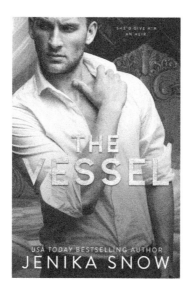

THE VESSEL

By Jenika Snow

www.JenikaSnow.com

Jenika_Snow@Yahoo.com

Copyright © July 2020 by Jenika Snow

First E-book Publication: July 2020

Photo provided by: Adobe Stock

Cover Designer: Lori Jackson

Editor: Kayla Robichaux

Create an heir or I lose the family business.

The final decree from my father on his deathbed, a millionaire who cared more about his business and money than what his son wanted in life, than if his son was happy.

I had a year to find a woman and convince her to have my baby or I'd lose everything. It was easy enough with the socialites who hung around in hopes I'd be with one of them.

But it would never happen.

I wanted a woman for my own, someone I could love, who could see past all my money and wanted me for me and not how I could advance their life. Yet at the end of the day, women only wanted me because I had deep pockets.

But then there was Elise. My employee. A

woman who I needed to keep a professional relationship with. I didn't see her as a means to an end. I saw her as the only woman who sparked life inside me with just a look. The only woman to have ever done that.

I hadn't desired someone in a long time, hadn't wanted a woman in my bed for longer than I'd admit.

I wanted to say screw it with my father's demand, and if that meant losing everything, so be it.

But could Elise be the one to give me everything? Happiness, love... a baby?

1

Lucius

"You have to be fucking kidding me." I didn't even bother censoring what I said.

Leave it to my father to fuck me over even from the grave.

I leaned back in the leather chair and stared at my father's attorney. Francis had been a bastard of a man to everyone he came in contact with, a God-awful father, and a possible sociopath if I really thought about it. But he'd been a brilliant business-man, could rub two pennies together and turn them into hundreds.

He showed me zero compassion and love while I'd been growing up, instead pawning me off on nannies and maids who raised me. He'd been a strict fucker, showed no remorse when I'd been a crying child because of his rants, but I guessed all of that shaped me into who I was today.

Since my father started Blacksmith, the brick-and-mortar consumer loan market company, a decade ago, I'd since taken over this avenue of the family business, so we now streamlined and incorporated it into an online venture. We can now help approve loans faster than banks. The success and hard work of Blacksmith now created a worth of 2.5 billion dollars.

He might not have been liked for his personality, or lack thereof, but people respected him, because he was a shark and legacy in what he did.

For many years, I felt sorry for him and myself. Because of him, I had a hard time connecting with people on an emotional and even personal level. It was hard for me to open up to anyone, to be real.

Another big "fuck you" from my father that would last me until the day I died.

"Theodore, please tell me this is a joke." My father passed away just last week, a heart attack taking him in the middle of the night. I'd been surprised I felt a twinge of sadness. But then I remembered Francis Blacksmith hadn't been a good man, especially to his only son.

The only form of affection I'd gotten had been from the nannies, even some of the estate staff who didn't have sticks up their asses thanks to my old man. But even then, they'd shown me kindness in secrecy, afraid of my father's wrath.

Because emotions signified weakness, and nobody got higher in life by not having a backbone. Or so he told me many times over.

My father didn't have a child out of love. He had a child so he'd have an heir to pass his company down to... so his name would never die.

And the bastard was forcing my hand on my personal life now.

"Mr. Blacksmith, although I admit the stipulations in your father's trust are quite... particular, unfortunately, they are ironclad in this instance."

I scoffed at the words coming from Theodore Jackson. I'd know my father's attorney for my entire life—thirty-seven long fucking years. Hell, I knew the only reason he was even still practicing was because my father made him. The old man would've been done and retired by now, probably would now, given the fact that there wasn't a threat of my father's rage hanging over his head.

"So what you're telling me, Theodore, is that I'm shit out of luck?"

Theodore pushed his thin, wire-rimmed glasses up his nose and pursed his lips, taking on a serious expression. "In so many words, Mr. Blacksmith, yes."

I looked past the attorney through his office windows, the city sprawling just on the other side of the glass. Lifting a hand, I ran my palm over the back of my head, no doubt mussing the short dark-blond strands.

In order for me to inherit anything, and I meant anything that was attached to the Blacksmith name, which I worked toward and built for decades, I had to produce an heir in a year's time. I didn't need a marriage of convenience, didn't even need anything more than a surrogate, according to my father's last words.

I just needed a biological heir.

If I got that, the Blacksmith fortune, the companies, the properties and everything that entailed, stayed mine. And if I failed... well, I lost everything.

As easy as it sounded, given the fact that there were enough money-hungry women who ran in my circles, ones who would be more than willing to give me what I wanted and be attached to the Blacksmith name in some form, this entire thing disgusted me.

I may have never saw myself finding a woman to spend the rest of my life with or have a family together. But that didn't mean I hadn't thought about it, wished that had been in my cards. My father had been a cold, heartless bastard. He might have engrained some of that apathetic nature in me through learned behavior, but the truth was, I'd love to have children, a wife who I loved, and the whole "dream" of being a family man.

So my options were pretty black-and-white.

Knock up a female to get that heir in twelve months.

Or kiss the Blacksmith legacy goodbye.

2

Elise

"No, no, no."

I clenched my teeth and refrained from snapping back at Merla, the "head housekeeper" for Lucius Blacksmith, which I knew she gave herself the title because there were no tiered employees working for the man. It wasn't like she got a raise by calling herself that, so I thought she was just a crusty old woman who was stuck in her way and wanted to make everyone follow her lead.

But she'd been here the longest, knew damn near everything, right down to how Mr. Blacksmith liked his coffee and at what time in the mornings, so everybody respected her and just fell in line. And I didn't want to ruffle feathers, so I did what I was told.

I might not have been here for very long in the grand scheme of things, but I was professional at every avenue, but I really didn't like someone berating me, even bitching about the way I polished the mahogany fireplace mantle.

I kept my mouth shut and just continued polishing. Merla was working behind me as we tag teamed Mr. Blacksmith's study.

When I first worked here and saw this room, it was instantly my favorite. Three out of four of the walls were nothing but built-in bookshelves, paperbacks and hardbacks lining the massive solid wood shelving. I'd always been an avid reader, and being here was like I'd fallen into the rabbit hole as if I were Alice. I didn't even care that almost all the books were about law or similar topics. I was just transfixed by it all.

I looked over my shoulder even as I continued polishing the mantle. Merla was busy working on the coffee table, her polishing meticulous. I had to give her credit, because she was damn good at what she did.

I glanced over at the bookshelves again, my secret love. More times than not, I thought about sneaking in here, grabbing one of the few non-law books, and sinking into the massive, distressed, brown leather loveseat that sat in front of the fireplace. I imagined curling up and letting the heat from the fire warm me on the outside, while a good book did the same on the inside.

When I saw Merla start to move away from the table, I quickly turned back around and focused on the mantle.

Once we were finished with the office, we made our way to the next room. Lucius Blacksmith's home was massive at three levels and a square footage that was no doubt in the five digits.

Why did one man need so much room? He wasn't married, had no children, and I'd never seen or heard of him with female companionship. He certainly never brought anyone back to the house, at least not when I was working. Maybe this was a family home? I only knew the bare basics of him from the staff, and of course the little I could find online. There was loads on the internet about his business life, but his personal side was almost non-existent.

But what everyone kept saying, what I kept reading, was that Lucius Blacksmith was one of the hottest, most eligible bachelors. And yeah, he really was.

I moved around the living room and started going to work there, and about twenty minutes later, I heard Mr. Blacksmith enter through the massive double front doors. I could hear his no doubt shined, expensive leather loafers padding over the granite foyer. His routine was always the same when he came home.

He set his large, heavy-looking suitcase by the door, the one that had his name embossed on the side, the lock at the top always gleaming gold as if he just polished it.

He hung up his suit jacket on the hook by the door then made his way into the kitchen, where I knew he poured himself a glass of scotch.

I made my way out of the living room with the small bucket of cleaning supplies. I lifted it up and pointed to the empty spray bottle, the natural concoction I personally mixed, a formula my grandmother taught my mom and my mother taught me.

It was a mixture of lavender, a few other essential oils, vinegar, water, and a couple other family secret ingredients that was so much better for the gorgeous, natural wood in Lucian's house, and it made me feel better knowing I wasn't using a bunch of chemicals.

Merla gave me a nod, as she understood what I was doing. She went back to cleaning.

The truth was, I had a whole full bottle in my bucket. I just wanted an excuse to check out Lucius. I liked seeing him in his suits when he got off work, the power that always surrounded him, but it seemed even more potent when he just got out of the office.

For months, I'd been lusting after my employer, but I wasn't stupid enough to tell anybody, to be unprofessional, or to be caught staring. Instead, I did things like pretend I needed to do a refill of the cleaning supplies.

I made my way into the kitchen and turned the corner to step into the room. The kitchen screamed of wealth and modern decor. Stainless steel appliances, white marble countertops, coordinating cupboards with rose gold accents. I didn't even want to think about how much all this actually cost.

I saw him before he saw me. Lucius Blacksmith and his intimidating form leaned against the counter. He had one foot crossed over the other, a palm braced on the counter beside him, and a bottle of beer in his free hand. On the granite next to him was a bottle of scotch, the cap facing up beside it, and an empty glass next to that. He tipped the bottle back and took a long pull from it, and as I stepped farther into the kitchen, my bucket hit the wall, causing a loud, echoing noise. That, in turn, had Lucius glancing over at me, the bottle still to his mouth, his eyes locked on me. His expression gave nothing away, just this stark, stoic mask covering his gorgeous, masculine face.

I gave him a small, polite smile, but inside I was a wreck, nervous as if I were under a microscope and he was examining me. I felt his eyes track my every move as I made my way over to the sink. I set the bucket on the counter, the bottles rattling around slightly. I chanced a look over at him; of course he still stared at me, probably wondering why I couldn't take my focus off him.

Lucius was a man in every sense of the word, exactly what I envisioned a real man was like. God, how he probably was in bed... how he'd take care of a woman in more ways than one.

"How is your evening going, Elise?"

I knew my eyes were wide. I felt them, like I was a deer caught in headlights, unable to do anything but be frozen in place. He knew my name. Sure, I'd been working for him for the past three months, but aside from a few small interactions, hellos or good-byes, good evening or good morning, Lucius didn't really speak with me. We shared plenty of pleasantries, but hell, even those didn't mean he knew every employee on his payroll. And, it wasn't like he hired me. Everything had gone through Merla.

I nodded. "Good. Thank you, Mr. Blacksmith." I hated that my voice betrayed my emotions. I felt my face heat because of that and quickly turned away from him to face the sink, trying to hide as much as I could.

For a moment, I forgot why I was even in the kitchen then realized I needed to "make another batch of cleaner." But I could still feel him watching me, his gaze heavy and thick, but I tried to ignore it despite the fact that I wouldn't be able to do the simplest of tasks right now because of him being so close.

I bent at the waist and opened up the cabinet underneath the sink, gathering what I'd need. I happened to glance over at him, and my breath left me when I saw where his focus was.

On my ass.

It's not like I was wearing anything remotely revealing or attractive. All the staff wore the same thing.

Either black slacks and a white cotton T-shirt, or a black knee-length dress with a white apron around the waist. I tried on the slacks at first, but the material felt restricting and itchy, so I just went with the dress, which was far easier for me to work in. And the fact that Mr. Blacksmith was staring at me—at that part of my body —had this flash of heat stealing over my entire body.

He slowly lifted his eyes to look up at me, and if I thought he'd act shamed or even guilty that he'd been caught checking me out, I was sorely mistaken. There wasn't one ounce of embarrassment over the fact that I caught him looking at my ass. Instead, he brought the bottle up to his mouth and finished it off as he stared me in the eyes, this heaviness coming from him.

I could have sworn he almost seemed... proud that I'd seen him.

"That's good you're doing well." His voice was so thick and deep. He set the empty beer bottle down on the counter and shoved his hands in the front pockets of his slacks.

God, he looked good in that dark suit, the white shirt underneath crisp, the red tie a contrast. He had the shirtsleeves rolled up his forearms, and I couldn't help but notice how muscular they were, vein-rippled, with a light sprinkling of dark-blond hair covering them.

I straightened and tried to breathe through this sudden arousal. If Merla saw me not doing work, she'd probably be pissed despite I was conversing with the boss. Merla was a stickler for procedure and professionalism; that was for sure. And I didn't think Lucius checking out my ass fell into that category.

I licked my lips and gave him another smile. "Thank you. I hope your day is going well too, Mr. Blacksmith."

"Call me, Lucius. Mr. Blacksmith was my father." His voice was deep and authoritative. I could picture him in a boardroom, commanding everyone with a simple string of words.

I wasn't sure what else to say, how to respond. For long seconds, we just stared at each other, this intense moment in which we held each other's gaze. It felt extremely... intimate.

"Elise, we need to start getting to work on the second level."

I heard Merla call out to me, and a second later, she stepped into the kitchen. I glanced over my shoulder at her, saw her posture stiffen as she took in Lucius standing just a couple feet from me. I looked over at him and saw he still watched me, paying no attention to the fact that we were no longer alone.

"My apologies, Mr. Blacksmith. Is Elise bothering you?"

I bristled at her tone and glanced at her. The fact that she implied me just being in his presence was some kind of hindrance pissed me off. I gnashed my teeth together, and when I cut my stare back to Lucius—his focus still on me—I could see a smirk start to form across his lips. It was clear I wasn't even trying to hide my annoyance.

"No, not at all. In fact, I'm very much enjoying her company."

I felt my cheeks heat once again and quickly put all the cleaning supplies back before putting what I needed in the bucket. I kept my head down and looked at him from under the fall of my lashes, suddenly feeling awkward and embarrassed, like a child who'd just gotten scolded.

"Have a good evening, Mr.... Lucius." I shouldn't have called him by his first name in front of Marla. She would most likely reprimand me, even if he told me to call him by that. But I felt a spark of rebellion, this pleasure that he wanted me to call him by his given name.

I wasn't one to break the rules or toe the line, and

certainly wasn't unprofessional, so the fact that I felt this way so instantly didn't sit well with me.

But as I made my way out of the kitchen, I still felt him watching me. And a look over my shoulder right before I turned the corner showed me I was right.

Lucius Blacksmith was checking out my ass again.

Available now on Amazon or read for FREE with a KU subscription!

ABOUT THE AUTHOR

Find Jenika at:

www.JenikaSnow.com

Jenika_Snow@yahoo.com

Made in the USA
Coppell, TX
26 March 2023